Everyone loves to read their horoscopes and have their fortunes told. Even me—and I *don't* happen to believe in fortune-tellers! As far as I'm concerned, they are all total fakes. So you can imagine my surprise when my best friend, Allie, went crazy for fortune-telling! Suddenly, quiet, sensible Allie was running to have her palm read or call her psychic advisor every time she had a decision to make.

But things really got out of hand when Allie decided to avoid her friends, and even cut school! She was headed for big trouble, and there was only one person who could help her. Me. I jumped right in with an absolutely perfect plan. Allie would be back to normal in no time—or so I thought. You know how it is with perfect plans. Somehow or other, they always seem to end up as total disasters! And this plan was no different. But before I explain how we got out of one big, bad-luck mess, let me tell you about something that *isn't* a disaster. My family. My very big family.

Right now there are nine people and a dog living in our house—and for all I know, someone new could move in at any time. There's me, my big sister, D.J., my little sister, Michelle, and my dad, Danny. But that's just the beginning.

When my mom died, Dad needed help. So he asked his old college buddy, Joey Gladstone, and my uncle Jesse to come live with us, to help take care of me and my sisters.

Back then, Uncle Jesse didn't know much about taking care of three little girls. He was more into rock 'n' roll. Joey didn't know anything about kids, either—but it sure was funny watching him learn!

Having Uncle Jesse and Joey around was like having three dads instead of one! But then something even better happened—Uncle Jesse fell in love. He married Becky Donaldson, Dad's co-host on his TV show, *Wake Up, San Francisco*. Aunt Becky's so nice—she's more like a big sister than an aunt.

Next Uncle Jesse and Aunt Becky had twin baby boys. Their names are Nicky and Alex, and they are adorable!

I love being part of a big family. Still, things can get pretty crazy when you live in such a full house!

FULL HOUSE™: Stephanie novels

FULL HOUSE™
Stephanie

Crazy About the Future

Devra Newberger Speregen

A Parachute Press Book

Published by POCKET BOOKS
New York   London   Toronto   Sydney   Tokyo   Singapore

This book is a work of fiction. Names, characters, places and incidents are products of the author's imagination or are used fictitiously. Any resemblance to actual events or locales or persons, living or dead, is entirely coincidental.

A MINSTREL PAPERBACK *Original*

 A Minstrel Book published by
POCKET BOOKS, a division of Simon & Schuster Inc.
1230 Avenue of the Americas, New York, NY 10020

A PARACHUTE PRESS BOOK

 READING Copyright © and ™ 1997 by Warner Bros.

ISBN: 0-671-00362-3

First Minstrel Books printing April 1997

10 9 8 7 6 5 4 3 2 1

Cover photo by Lisa Rose/Globe Photos, Inc.

Printed in the U.S.A.

Crazy About the Future

CHAPTER
1

◆ ◀ ◢ ◆

Stephanie Tanner closed one eye and pushed her long blond hair behind her ears. She aimed at the six bottles that were stacked in a pyramid on the tabletop. She tightened her grip around the softball in her hand and pulled her arm way back. Then she threw the ball as hard as she could.

Whack!

A direct hit! All six bottles flew off the table and crashed to the ground.

"Yahoo, Stephanie!" Allie Taylor cheered. Allie was Stephanie's best friend. She had soft, wavy brown hair and green eyes. "You did it! You won!" Allie smiled, then clapped a hand over her mouth. Allie recently got braces, and she was still shy about letting them show.

"Way to go, Steph!" cried Darcy Powell, Stephanie's other best friend. Darcy grinned. Darcy had also gotten braces recently, but she wasn't the least bit shy about them. Darcy pulled her wavy dark hair back into a gold scrunchie.

"Why don't you take a turn, Allie?" Darcy asked.

"Yeah," Stephanie agreed. "You have pretty good aim."

"Forget it," Allie told her. "The way my luck is going lately, I'd probably miss the bottles and hit—him!" Allie pointed at the redheaded guy behind the carnival booth.

Stephanie and Darcy giggled.

"Seriously, Al, don't let it get you down," Stephanie said. "So, a few bad things have happened to you lately."

"A few bad things?" Allie said. "First, I lost my big English term paper."

"But you wrote it again," Darcy reminded her. "And still handed it in on time."

"Yeah, but I already threw out my notes," Allie said. "I forgot to write the most important part of the paper, and I got a terrible grade."

2

"Well, that could happen to anyone," Stephanie told her.

"Maybe," Allie said. "But then I was talking to Josh Trumbull, and I lifted my arm to point at something—and split the seam on my brand-new tunic top!" Allie groaned.

Stephanie and Darcy exchanged sympathetic looks. Allie was kind of shy, especially around cute guys like Josh Trumbull. They knew how embarrassed she must have been.

"Plus this morning I broke my mother's most favorite vase. She acted really nice about it, but I know she was upset," Allie finished.

"Well, everybody has a run of bad luck sometimes," Darcy said.

"Not like this," Allie grumbled. "I wish I knew how to stop it."

"Don't worry. I'm sure it's already over," Stephanie told her.

"Hey!" the redheaded guy in the booth called to Stephanie. "Don't you want your prize?" he asked.

"Sure! I can't wait to see it," Stephanie said.

"Here it is." The guy handed her a tiny pink stuffed rabbit. It was only about three inches tall and it was missing some whiskers.

Stephanie stared at the scruffy rabbit. "This is it?" she asked in amazement. "This is my big prize?"

The guy laughed. "What were you expecting?" he asked. "A million dollars?"

Stephanie rolled her eyes. "Let's try some other game. Or maybe another ride," she said.

Stephanie, Darcy, and Allie hurried away from the booth. Stephanie stuffed the toy rabbit into her backpack. "Maybe I'll give this to Nicky," she said. Nicky was her four-year-old cousin. He collected stuffed animals.

"Sure, he'll love it," Darcy said. She reached up and patted her dainty gold hoop earrings. A small pearl dangled from each hoop.

"Don't worry, Darce," Stephanie teased. "Your earrings are still there."

Darcy laughed. "Sorry! I just can't stop touching them. You know my grandma only gave them to me yesterday. And I love them so much. They're the nicest earrings I ever had."

"They look great on you," Stephanie told her.

"And they look especially nice with your hair pulled back, too," Allie added.

"So . . . where to now, guys?" Stephanie asked.

4

"How about the roller coaster?" Darcy suggested.

"No way!" Allie joked. "I'm afraid I might fall out!"

"Let's just walk around until we see something new to do," Stephanie suggested. She glanced at her watch. "We don't have to meet my dad yet. We have forty-five minutes till it's time to go home."

Darcy and Allie agreed, so they strolled through the carnival and checked out the scene. The carnival came to Golden Gate Park in San Francisco every year. Stephanie loved going. She loved strolling under the bright strings of lights on the arcade. She loved the excitement of all the colorful booths and the crowds of people hurrying from one ride to another. She loved the sounds of the carnival barkers trying to get people to play the games of chance. She even loved the cotton candy and the hot dogs.

It was too bad that the carnival only ran for two weeks. Stephanie usually went with her family on the first night, but this year she asked Allie and Darcy to come along, too.

"Hey, Stephanie," Allie asked as they walked,

"did you decide on a topic for your *Scribe* article yet?"

"No." Stephanie sighed and shook her head. She'd been trying to come up with a good idea for the school paper all week. "Do you guys have any ideas?" she asked.

"What about an article about my bad luck?" Allie suggested.

"Oh, that would be real interesting," Stephanie joked.

"You haven't thought of anything at all?" Darcy asked.

Stephanie shook her head. "No. I was kind of hoping to do a real investigative piece," she said. "You know, like when a reporter goes under-cover to expose some criminal activity."

"You mean like on those TV shows, where they use hidden cameras to catch people making up a secret plot or something?" Allie asked.

Darcy shook her head. "That's nothing new," she said. "Stephanie already did that kind of article. Remember? When she tried to expose the bad food in the school cafeteria."

"Who could forget that?" Allie asked.

Stephanie grinned. "Especially when I

couldn't find any secret plots and ended up writing about meat loaf instead," she said.

They all laughed. Stephanie felt lucky to have two such good friends. She had met Allie on her first day of kindergarten, and they were best friends ever since. They were a lot alike. For instance, they both loved music and reading.

Darcy had met Stephanie and Allie in the sixth grade. Darcy's family had moved to San Francisco from Chicago. Darcy had tons of energy. She was also bright and funny, and a very good athlete. Stephanie, Darcy, and Allie always had a great time when they did things together—when they could decide *what* to do, that is!

"Hey!" Darcy called. "Check this out." She pointed to a purple carnival tent. Across the front of the tent hung a big sign. It read: ESTHER'S TENT OF WONDER. FORTUNES TOLD. PALMS READ.

"Wow, a fortune-teller!" Allie exclaimed. "Maybe she could tell me if my bad luck will last forever."

"Oh, come on," Stephanie scoffed. "Fortune-tellers aren't real. They just make up stories to tell people."

"Well, it only costs seventy-five cents," Allie said. "Let's just try it."

"Why not? It could be fun," Darcy agreed. She headed toward the tent.

Stephanie grabbed Darcy's arm. "Are you guys serious? It sounds like a waste of money to me. Let's play more arcade games instead."

"I'd really like to check out Esther's Tent of Wonder," Allie said.

"Yeah! Maybe my palm says that I'm going to win a lot of money," Darcy added. "Come on, Steph. Let's just try it."

Stephanie rolled her eyes. "But it's silly!"

"I don't know about that," Allie said. "Once I got a fortune cookie that said, 'Good fortune comes to those who search.'"

"So?" Stephanie asked.

"So that same night, I was searching through my pockets for change, and I found a five-dollar bill," Allie told her.

"Really?" Darcy asked. "That is so cool!"

"But it doesn't prove that the fortune was true," Stephanie told her. "Once I went for Chinese food with my family, and my fortune cookie said, 'You have the brains in the family.'"

"So what's wrong with that?" Allie asked.

"My whole family got the exact same fortune," Stephanie replied. "Even Comet, the dog!"

Darcy and Allie laughed.

"Well, I still want to check out Esther's Tent of Wonder," Allie said. "I'm serious, Steph. This bad luck is driving me crazy. Maybe Esther can help."

Stephanie sighed. "Oh, all right. I'll go," she said. "But don't expect me to get my palm read. I don't believe in fortunes!"

CHAPTER

2

◆ ◀ ◆ ◆

Allie pushed open the entrance flaps to Esther's Tent of Wonder. "Wow!" she exclaimed. "Check out this place!"

Stephanie peered inside. She had to admit, it *was* pretty wild. There were colorful scarves and wind chimes hanging from the ceiling of the tent. The tent was lit up with purple lightbulbs that made the chimes and scarves glow purple, too. A large table stood in the middle of the room. A gleaming crystal ball perched on the tabletop.

A pretty young woman sat in front of the crystal ball. She wore a flowing pink-and-purple robe with wide sleeves. A matching purple scarf was tied around her head, over her shoulder-length brown hair. Huge gold hoop earrings dangled from her ears, and her wrists were nearly covered with stacks of thin, gold bangle bracelets.

"Wow, she looks incredible," Allie whispered.

"She does look pretty amazing," Stephanie whispered back. "Hello," the woman called to them. "I'm Esther. Please, come in and sit down." She pointed to three chairs set around the table. Her bracelets jingled loudly.

"Can you really predict the future?" Allie asked as she sat down. "Because I'm having this streak of bad luck, and—"

Stephanie rolled her eyes. "Don't tell her that!" she exclaimed. "If she's a real fortune-teller, she should know it already."

Esther grinned. "Well, I'm not a mind reader," she said. "But ask me anything you want to know."

Stephanie narrowed her eyes. "I'd like to know if you can tell me what I ate for dinner tonight."

Esther waved her arms above her crystal ball. She closed her eyes. "Yes!" she said. "I see it as clear as day. You ate a hot dog for dinner!"

Allie and Darcy exchanged surprised looks.

"That's right!" Allie said in amazement. "She

11

did eat a hot dog! And you saw that in your crystal ball?"

"No," Esther told them. "I saw that on her jacket. There's a big mustard stain on the sleeve."

Stephanie's face turned red. Darcy and Allie cracked up. "That's a good one," Darcy told Esther.

Esther smiled. "But let's get serious now," she added. "If you like, I can look into my crystal ball or at my special fortune-telling cards and tell you what I *really* see."

"Definitely!" Allie reached into her pocket and pulled out three quarters.

Stephanie folded her arms across her chest. "This is silly, Allie," she whispered.

Esther took the money and dropped it into her robe pocket. Then she produced a box of large, odd-looking cards and began to shuffle them. She pushed the deck toward Allie.

Esther asked Allie to cut the cards once or twice. Finally she set the stack of cards in the center of the table. "Turn over one card, please," she told Allie.

Allie flipped over the top card. It showed a picture of some flowers and two birds. Esther studied the card and then studied Allie. She touched the card. "This card suggests that you are an animal lover," Esther told Allie. "You have deep feelings for *all* animals."

Allie's jaw dropped open. "That's amazing!" she cried. "I *am* an animal lover!"

"That's true," Darcy said. "These cards are incredible." Darcy turned to Stephanie. "Don't you agree?"

"Well, that could have been a lucky guess," Stephanie replied.

Darcy shrugged. She turned to Esther. "Can I pick a card?" she asked.

"Of course." Esther shuffled again and asked Darcy to turn over a card. Darcy chose one from the center of the deck. It showed a picture of a strange-looking girl running as if something were chasing her.

Stephanie leaned forward to get a better look at the card. She glanced at Allie and Darcy. They were both holding their breath as they watched Esther. Esther studied the card in silence.

"You are a great athlete. A competitor who likes to win," Esther said.

Darcy's eyes widened. "That's right," she said. "I am. I play tennis and field hockey. I'm in competitions all the time, and I *love* to win!"

"Right again!" Allie said.

Esther nodded at Stephanie. "Would you like to try?" she asked.

"Sorry," Stephanie replied. "I don't really believe in fortune-telling."

Esther grinned. "Is that *completely* true?" she asked.

"Sure. I mean, I guess so," Stephanie answered. She flushed. Esther's dark eyes stared straight into her own. Stephanie felt a little embarrassed. "I mean, I guess I read fortunes in fortune cookies sometimes. But I don't take it too seriously," she added.

Esther smiled. "So, you're not a believer," she said. "That's okay. Fortune-telling isn't for everyone."

"Well, it's fine for me," Allie announced. "But I have more questions. Esther, will you read my palm? I really need to know what's going to happen in my future."

Allie pulled another seventy-five cents from her pocket and put the coins on the table. Then she held out her hand. Esther grasped it and studied both sides. She spent a long time staring at Allie's palm.

"Hmmm, this is very interesting," Esther finally remarked. She pointed to a crease running across

14

the width of Allie's hand. "This is your good-fortune line," Esther told her. "See how long it is?"

"Yes," Allie said. "That's good, isn't it! So why am I having so much bad luck?"

Esther smiled at her. "Well, do you see this other crease—the one that crosses your good-fortune line?"

"I see it," Allie said. "It's long, too."

"Well, not *too* long," Esther said. "But this is your adverse-fortune line. That means something like bad luck."

Allie groaned. "I knew it! My bad-fortune line is nearly as long as my *good*-fortune line. No wonder everything's going wrong for me lately!"

"Oh, Allie!" Darcy said. "That's terrible!"

"Don't worry," Esther assured them. "Everyone has 'bad' fortune in their lives. It doesn't have to be terrible. In fact, many people believe you need 'bad' luck to make you appreciate your good luck even more."

"You're just saying that to make me feel better," Allie said.

"Well, many people really think it's true," Esther said. She leaned over Allie's palm again and frowned. Esther glanced quickly at Allie. "Do you happen to have a big test coming up soon?'' she asked.

''Yes, a history test,'' Allie replied.

Esther nodded. ''That could be the one,'' she said.

''What one?'' Allie asked. She looked panicky. ''Is that part of my bad luck?''

Esther shrugged. ''It might be. You had better be well prepared.''

''Can't you tell her about something good?'' Stephanie asked. She was beginning to worry that Esther would make Allie even more upset about her ''bad luck'' than before!

''I can only say what I see,'' Esther said. She studied Allie's hand again. ''You should be careful on the sixteenth of this month,'' she said. ''Especially around groups of people.''

''The sixteenth? That's Monday,'' Allie said. ''Is something really bad going to happen to me on Monday?''

''It could,'' Esther said. ''It might just mean that someone will trip you accidentally, or you might stub your toe. Or it could be something worse.''

''Oh,'' Allie said. She tried to smile.

''Wow. That's amazing. What about me?''

Darcy asked. She held out her hand, too. "Do you see any bad stuff on my palm?"

Esther studied Darcy's palm. "Hmmm. Your good-fortune line is also very long," she said. "In fact, I see a big win in your future."

Darcy's eyes danced in excitement. "Really? Because I have a big tennis match coming up soon," she said. "Will *that* be my big win?"

"It could be," Esther replied.

Darcy ignored Esther's answer. "Wow! How cool is that? I'm going to win my tennis match!"

Esther's expression turned serious. "Don't forget about your adverse-fortune line," she said. "As I told your friend, everyone's life includes both good and bad fortune," Esther went on. "Don't be upset, but I see that you will also have a big loss."

Darcy frowned. "Well, *that's* not good." She stared at her hand and rubbed her bad-fortune line.

"What about you, nonbeliever?" Esther asked Stephanie.

Stephanie sat up straighter in her chair. "Who, me?" she asked.

Esther nodded. "Yes. What if I gaze into my crystal ball and tell you what I see?" she asked.

"I don't think a crystal ball can really show pictures of my future," Stephanie replied.

"Well, the crystal ball isn't magic or anything," Esther said. "But it *does* set a nice mood in my tent," she teased.

Stephanie laughed. She had to admit, Esther was funny.

Esther smiled at Stephanie. "Why don't you let me read your palm?"

"No, thanks. Really," Stephanie said. "I already know my future. In about two seconds, I'm leaving this tent." She stood up and headed for the exit.

"Wait!" Esther called after her. "I'll make a prediction, anyway. Maybe it will change your mind about fortune-telling."

Stephanie paused in the doorway. She turned around. "Okay," she agreed. "Just one little prediction."

Esther closed her eyes and hummed softly to herself. She opened her eyes.

"My prediction is this," Esther announced in a dramatic voice. "You will soon hold the key to your family's happiness!"

CHAPTER
3

♦ ◀ ◣ ♦

Allie and Darcy followed Stephanie out of Esther's tent.

"The key to my family's happiness? That is totally silly," Stephanie said. She laughed. "Right, guys?"

"Maybe." Allie paused. "Actually, I'm a little worried about what she said. Especially about having my bad luck in groups of people. Monday the sixteenth isn't far away," she said.

Stephanie stared at Allie. "You *are* kidding, I hope."

"No, I'm not," Allie replied. "In fact, I just made up my mind. I'm not going to school on

Monday. That's the only time I'm around large groups of people, right?''

"Right," Darcy said.

"So I'll stay home," Allie declared. "Then, if it really *is* my unlucky day, I'll be safe."

"You can't stay home from school," Stephanie said. "What would you tell your parents?"

"I don't know yet," Allie said. "Maybe I won't tell them anything. Maybe I'll pretend I'm sick. I could even get ready for school, then hide in the backyard until they both leave for work."

"Allie! That's cutting!" Darcy exclaimed in horror.

"And you never cut a day of school in your life!" Stephanie added. She and Darcy exchanged looks of concern.

"Stephanie's right, Al," Darcy said. "You can't just cut school now, for no reason."

"Esther's prediction is a big reason," Allie told her. "It's definite. There's no way I'm going to go to school on Monday."

"Allie, please don't do it," Stephanie begged. "What if you get in big trouble? And all because of something that might or *might not* happen!"

"But what if Esther is right?" Allie asked.

"What if something terrible is going to happen to me?"

"Allie, nothing terrible will happen to you," Stephanie said. "Esther doesn't know everything."

"Really?" Allie asked. "Then how did she know about me being an animal lover? Or about Darcy being an athlete?"

Stephanie shrugged. "I don't know. Maybe those were lucky guesses," she replied. "Right, Darcy?"

Darcy looked confused. "Well, maybe," she said. "I mean, after all, *some* of what she said was true."

Stephanie frowned. "But no one can *really* predict the future."

Allie shook her head. "I'm not so sure, Steph. I mean, I always read my horoscope in the newspaper, and lots of times it comes true."

"Yes, but—" Stephanie began.

"Oh, no!" Darcy suddenly cried. "Oh, no! It's *gone!*"

Stephanie spun around toward Darcy. "What's gone? What happened?"

Darcy shook out her school varsity jacket. She pulled off her hair scrunchie and ran her fingers through her hair.

21

"Where is it?" Darcy wailed. She dropped onto her hands and knees and began frantically searching the ground. "My earring is gone!" Darcy wailed. Her eyes welled up with tears. "The left one is missing. It must have just fallen out. I know it was there a second ago."

Stephanie and Allie immediately fell to their knees to help search for the earring.

"When was the last time you're sure you had it on?" Allie asked.

Darcy thought hard. "I know I had it when we left Esther's tent."

"Yeah, I remember seeing it then," Stephanie agreed.

"What am I going to do? I can't tell my grandma. She'll think I can't be trusted with nice things," Darcy said. "And my mom told me not to wear these earrings tonight. She said I should save them for special occasions."

"Maybe we'll find it," Stephanie told her.

They retraced their steps, but they didn't see the earring anywhere.

"I'm sorry, Darce, but it's time to meet my family for our ride home," Stephanie finally said.

"I guess we better go," Allie added.

"Oh, no. I hate to give up. This is just terrible!" Darcy wailed. "I loved these earrings so much!"

Stephanie put an arm around her. "Don't worry, Darce," she said. "Let's call the carnival in the morning. I'm sure they have a lost and found. Maybe someone will find your earring and turn it in."

"Oh, no!" Allie gasped. Stephanie and Darcy whirled around.

"Now what? Did you lose something, too?" Stephanie asked.

Allie shook her head. "No—but I just realized something incredible!"

"What?" Darcy asked.

"It's Esther!" Allie replied. "She was right!"

Stephanie felt confused. "What are you talking about?"

"It's the 'big loss,' " Allie explained. "Darcy lost her brand-new earring! Don't you see? Part of Esther's prediction already came true!"

"Wow. That is really spooky," Darcy said.

Allie turned to Stephanie. "I told you Esther was for real," she said. "You have to believe her now, Steph."

Stephanie swallowed hard. "But, Allie, that's silly," she replied. "It could be just a coinci-

Full House: Stephanie

dence. Darcy was bound to lose something she
owned sooner or later. It could have been a pen-
cil, or even a phone number."

Allie shook her head. "I don't believe that,"
she said. "Esther said that Darcy would lose
something important. And her new earring *was*
important to her." Allie's expression was grim.
"That settles it. I am definitely cutting school on
the sixteenth."

"But, Allie, cutting school is bad luck, too,"
Stephanie tried to argue.

"Forget it, Steph," Allie told her. "You can't
talk me out of this."

Stephanie gazed at Darcy. "Darcy, help me.
Talk to her!" she pleaded.

Darcy gave a helpless shrug. "I'm not sure
what to say," she admitted.

Stephanie sighed. She checked her watch.
"Yikes! We're really late now. My dad will have
a fit if he has to wait any longer. Come on,
guys."

Danny Tanner, Stephanie's father, believed in
being on time for everything.

"Okay," Darcy said. She took one last look
around on the ground. Then she and Allie followed Stephanie toward the parking lot.

"That earring won't turn up in any lost and found," Allie whispered to Stephanie. "It's gone forever. I'm sorry you don't believe in fortune-telling, Steph, because I think Esther just proved that you *can* predict the future."

"But, Allie—" Stephanie began to say. She glanced up and spotted her father.

Danny Tanner was pacing up and down beside the family's van. He didn't look happy. Neither did the rest of her family—except for her little cousins.

Four-year-old Nicky ran toward her.

"Hey, Cousin Stephanie!" Nicky cried. "Guess what? We went on the roller coaster with Daddy!"

"You did?" Stephanie asked, trying to look as amazed as possible.

Nicky's twin brother, Alex, ran up to her, too. Alex jumped up and down. "And I ate cotton!" he yelled.

"That's cotton *candy*," Stephanie's uncle Jesse corrected him.

"Sounds like you guys had major fun," Stephanie told the twins. "But what happened to you, Michelle?" she asked her younger sister. "Why do you look so green?"

Nine-year-old Michelle sprawled on the ground of the parking lot. She clutched her stomach and groaned.

"Uh, Michelle can't talk right now," Joey Gladstone told Stephanie. Joey lived with the Tanners. He was Danny Tanner's best friend back in college.

"What's wrong with Michelle?" Stephanie asked.

"I guess eating two slices of pizza before going on the Tilting Teacup ride made her kind of sick," Joey explained.

Michelle groaned again.

Danny glanced at his watch. "You're very late, Stephanie," he scolded.

"Sorry, Dad," Stephanie replied.

"It's my fault, Mr. Tanner," Darcy told him. "I lost an earring, and Steph and Allie were helping me look for it."

"Oh, I'm sorry, Darcy," Danny said.

"Thanks," Darcy answered. She looked so sad that Stephanie felt sorry for her all over again.

"Maybe someone will find it and turn it in," Becky told Darcy.

"I hope so, too," Jesse said. He zipped up his

black leather jacket. "Brrr," he said. "It's starting to get cold, Danny. What are we going to do about going home?"

"Huh? Why don't we just get in the van and drive home?" Stephanie asked.

Danny looked embarrassed. "Well, actually, we have a little problem with the car keys," he told her.

"Really, Dad? But you always keep your keys in the same place—your right-hand pants pocket," Stephanie said. "You didn't lose them, did you?"

Danny's face turned red. "Of course I didn't lose the keys! I know exactly where they are."

Danny pointed into the van. "They're right there," he said. "Inside the car. I locked them in by mistake."

Joey groaned. "You mean, you locked us *out* by mistake," he said.

"Well, one of us better go call a locksmith," Jesse said.

"But it might take a really long time for a locksmith to get here," Danny pointed out.

Jesse hugged his arms to his chest to keep warm. "Yeah, but do you have a better idea?" he asked.

"Well, I—" Danny began to say.

Michelle groaned again. "I don't feel so good. I want to go home!" she cried.

"Mommy! I want to go home, too!" Nicky wailed.

"Me too! Alex cried.

Becky sighed. Becky was the twins' mom. She also worked with Stephanie's dad on their morning television show, *Wake Up, San Francisco*. "We'll be going home soon, guys. As soon as your uncle Danny admits he messed up and—"

"I did not mess up!" Danny insisted. "I was under a lot of stress today and I—"

"Stop it, you guys! Arguing won't help!" Stephanie exclaimed. "What a night! First Darcy loses her earring, and now this."

"That's funny," Allie said. "Esther didn't predict that your *dad* would lose anything."

"Esther? Who's Esther?" Becky asked.

"This amazing fortune-teller," Allie said.

Stephanie made a face. "Allie, please don't start talking about Esther again," she said. "That won't help a bit."

"Now I'm freezing," Michelle complained.

"Here, Michelle," Stephanie said, taking off

her jacket. "Put on my jacket. It's warmer than yours."

Stephanie tossed her denim jacket to Michelle. As it flew through the air a key chain dropped out of the pocket and hit the ground.

"What's this?" she said, picking it up. "This isn't my key."

"Hey! Let me see that!" Jesse said. He bent over and studied the key in her hand. "It's a spare key for the van!"

Joey cheered. "Hooray! We're not locked out anymore!"

Stephanie's eyes widened. "You're kidding!" she said.

Danny walked over to inspect the key. "Yup. That's it," he said. Then he looked at Stephanie. "What are you doing with a key to the van? You don't even drive."

Stephanie stared at the key in her hand, feeling confused. "I have no idea," she replied. "I didn't put it in my jacket."

"Aha!" Allie exclaimed. Everyone turned to stare at her.

"What? What is it this time?" Stephanie asked.

"Esther was right again!" Allie declared.

29

"Please, Allie," Stephanie said. "Who cares about Esther at a time like this?"

Allie folded her arms across her chest and gloated. "Uh, maybe you should, Stephanie. Because I think you've forgotten Esther's last prediction." Allie took a deep breath. "You are now holding the *key* to your family's happiness!"

CHAPTER
4

◆ ◀ ▸ ◆

Allie leaned across the table. "Okay, then how do you explain about you having that car key Wednesday night?" she demanded.

Allie, Stephanie, and Darcy sat together in the Food Court at the mall. It was Saturday, and they had just spent two hours shopping. Allie was the only one who had actually spent any money. Stephanie and Darcy had watched her pay over twenty dollars for good-luck charms and books about superstitions and fortune-telling in a new store called The Four-Leaf Clover.

Stephanie put down her egg roll and stared back at Allie. "I told you a million times, Allie, me finding that key was a coincidence!" she said. "There's a logical explanation for the whole thing. D.J. wore my denim jacket the other night when she went to the library. She left the key in my jacket pocket."

"But Esther was *still* right about the key," Allie insisted. "And she was right about Darcy's big loss. Don't forget about that!"

Darcy reached up to rub her bare earlobe. "Don't remind me," she said.

"Sorry, Darce," Allie said. She helped herself to more rice and some sweet-and-sour chicken. They were sharing three orders of Chinese food for lunch.

Allie pulled a book out of her shopping bag. She flipped through the pages, read something, and put the book down. "None of that chicken for me," Allie said. "My new book of daily predictions says I should keep my life very simple today."

"What's that got to do with eating chicken?" Stephanie asked.

"This book says its predictions affect every part of your life," Allie explained. "That means what you wear, what you do, even what you eat.

And sweet-and-sour chicken isn't simple food, so I don't want to eat it," Allie added.

Darcy stared at her in disbelief. "Won't you be hungry?" Darcy asked.

"No. I'll have plenty of plain white rice. That's very simple food," Allie said. "Oh, Steph, are you using your spoon?" she asked.

"No. You can use it," Stephanie said. She handed it to Allie. Allie scooped a huge helping of rice onto her plate. Then she began eating the rice with the spoon.

Stephanie and Darcy exchanged startled looks. "Uh, Allie, why aren't you eating with a fork?" Stephanie asked.

"Because my horoscope in the newspaper this morning said to beware of sharp objects," Allie answered.

Stephanie groaned. "Listen, Allie," she said. "I thought we agreed that you wouldn't go overboard with all these horoscopes and predictions."

"But I'm not going overboard," Allie replied. "I'm just playing it safe."

Stephanie reached into her backpack and drew out a notebook. "But look at this," she said. She flipped open the notebook and showed Allie a chart. "We all agreed to follow our horoscopes and see if they came true or not, right?"

"Right," Allie replied.

"Well, here's my list," Stephanie said. "I've been tracking my horoscope for three days. And only one horoscope came true."

"Which one?" Allie said.

"The one that said I'd receive good news about money, and I found out that I didn't owe a fine on my library book," Stephanie said.

"And we're not even sure if the horoscope meant the library book," Darcy added. "It could have meant almost anything."

"Well, I kept track of my horoscopes, too," Allie said. "And mine *all* came true."

"I don't believe that," Stephanie told her.

"Me either," Darcy said. "Most of my horoscopes were so unclear, I couldn't tell if they came true or not."

Allie shook her head in impatience. "But I *do* think they come true."

"Maybe they do, sometimes," Stephanie told her. "We just don't want you to take this stuff so seriously *all* the time."

"Well, I *am* taking them seriously," Allie replied. "Especially Esther's predictions. And I am definitely staying home from school on Monday."

"You're crazy if you do," Stephanie warned. "Do you know how much trouble you'll be in if you get caught?"

"Less trouble than if I go to school on an unlucky day!" Allie replied. "I'm not taking any chances, Steph. Not until all this bad luck is over."

"Allie, I don't want to argue about it," Stephanie said. "It's just that I'm worried about you." She pointed to the large shopping bag that rested on the floor next to Allie's feet.

"For instance, don't you think you went a little overboard, buying all this fortune-telling stuff? I mean, those things you bought cost a fortune."

"They're just basics, and they weren't expensive," Allie replied.

"Books, crystals, cards . . . those are basics?" Stephanie asked.

"First of all, these are called *tarot* cards. They're an ancient tool for telling fortunes," Allie corrected her. Her face turned slightly red. "And it's my allowance for the month, Stephanie, so I can do whatever I want with it."

Stephanie was silent for a minute. "Allie, do

you *really* think that keeping a black rock that cost five dollars in your pocket will raise your grade in English?''

"That's what the saleslady promised," Allie pointed out.

"She didn't promise," Darcy said. "She just said that the rock is called hematite, and that hematite may give you knowledge and understanding."

Stephanie took a deep breath. "What about the three-dollar red rock?"

"That's for power and strength," Allie replied.

"And the crystals?" Stephanie asked.

"They ward off evil," Allie replied.

"So she'll be strong enough to fight off evil spells when she lifts her new set of encyclopedias," Darcy joked.

Neither Allie nor Stephanie laughed.

"Come on, you guys," Darcy said. "Let's drop it. All we talk about lately is fortunes and horoscopes. Let's change the subject."

"Okay." Stephanie turned to Allie. "What movie should we see tonight?" she asked. "How about that new one about aliens invading the earth?"

"Ugh!" Darcy said. "I was hoping to see the

new Tom Cruise movie. You guys both love Tom Cruise."

"Which will it be, Allie? Aliens or Tom?" Stephanie asked.

Allie stared down at her food. "Actually, I don't think I can go out with you guys tonight," she muttered.

Darcy put down her egg roll. "Why not?" she asked.

"It's just . . . well . . . okay, if you must know, it's Anna," Allie said.

Stephanie and Darcy exchanged puzzled looks.

"Who's Anna?" Stephanie asked.

"She's my new friend at The Psychic Hot Line," Allie answered. "When I spoke to her this morning, she told me that tonight holds bad karma for me."

Stephanie raised her eyebrows. "Bad karma?" she asked.

"Yeah, that's kind of like bad luck," Allie explained. "Anna warned me to stay close to home tonight." Then her eyes lit up. "But Sunday is a *good* karma day all day. So if you guys can wait until tomorrow to see a movie, I'll go with you."

Stephanie stared at Allie in disbelief. "Since

when does this Anna tell you what to do?" she asked.

"Well, since Wednesday night, after the carnival. I've called her every day since then," Allie said. "I've done exactly what she said so far—and I think my bad luck is getting better."

Stephanie turned to Darcy. "Am I crazy, or is this the most ridiculous thing you've ever heard?" she asked.

"Well, I—" Darcy began to reply.

Allie leaped up from the table. She grabbed her shopping bag from the floor. "Look, Stephanie, I don't have to listen to you making fun of me for the rest of the day. I'm sorry if you don't take my bad luck seriously, but I do. So I'm going home now. I'll see you guys in school. On *Tuesday*." Allie stormed away.

Stephanie and Darcy stared after her in shock.

"We have to do something!" Stephanie finally exclaimed. "What if Allie starts cutting school whenever Anna says she'll have bad karma?"

"This is really getting out of hand," Darcy agreed. "I had no idea she was calling those telephone psychics. You know how much money those calls are. She'll go broke!" Stephanie snapped her fingers. "I've got it! Forget the movie tonight. We're going back to the carnival instead!"

"We are?" Darcy asked in surprise. "Why?"

"To see Esther," Stephanie replied. "Maybe we can get her to change what she said about the sixteenth being bad luck. Then we can convince Allie to give up all this fortune-telling stuff," she told Darcy. Stephanie stood up and slung her backpack over her shoulder. "So, can you come with me?" she asked.

"Hmm?" Darcy mumbled. She stared at a small piece of paper in her hand.

"I said, can you come with me tonight," Stephanie repeated.

"Sure. It's fate anyway," Darcy said. "We weren't meant to go to a movie tonight."

"What do you mean?" Stephanie asked.

Darcy held out her hand. Resting on her palm was a fortune from a fortune cookie. Darcy read the fortune out loud: "Tonight be prepared for a change of plans!"

CHAPTER
5

◆ ◀ ▸ ◆

Back at home, Stephanie raced up to D.J.'s bedroom. "Hey, Deej!" she called. "Can you give us a ride to the carnival?" She peered into the room. It was empty. Michelle appeared in the hall, coming up the stairs.

"D.J.'s not home," Michelle explained when she saw Stephanie at D.J.'s door. "She had to meet her study group for some big project or something."

"Oh. Well, is Dad home yet?" Stephanie asked.

"Dad and Joey went to see the new Tom Cruise movie," Michelle told her. "I wanted to go, but I still feel sick from last night."

Stephanie groaned. "You mean, D.J., Dad, *and* Joey are out for the whole night?"

There go three possible drivers, she thought.

"How about Uncle Jesse and Aunt Becky? Are they home?" she asked.

Michelle nodded. "Yup. Aunt Becky is in the backyard with the twins. Uncle Jesse is upstairs."

Stephanie raced up the steps to the attic apartment. She knocked on the door. "Uncle Jesse?" she called out. "Got a minute?"

There was no answer.

"Uncle Jesse?"

Still no reply. Stephanie turned the knob and walked inside. Uncle Jesse was lying on the sofa. An open book covered his face.

"Uncle Jesse?" she said again.

Jesse sat up abruptly, sending the book crashing to the floor. He quickly scooped it up and held it up in front of his eyes.

"Uh, I'm just, uh, finishing up this chapter," he said, trying to hide a yawn. Then he realized he was talking to Stephanie.

"Oh, it's just you, Steph!" He breathed a sigh of relief and tossed the book on the sofa. "I thought you were Becky."

Stephanie stared at him. "Why would you tell

41

Becky you were reading?'' she asked. She knew Uncle Jesse had been sleeping. ''What book is that, anyway?'' she added.

Jesse rubbed his eyes. *''The Tale of the Willow Tree,''* he replied.

''Oh, by Charles Frost,'' Stephanie said.

Jesse's eyes opened wide in amazement. ''You mean you've heard of it?'' he asked.

Stephanie laughed. ''Heard of it? I had to read it last year for English class.''

Jesse's eyes widened more. ''You've *read* it?'' he asked. ''The whole thing?''

''Yeah, why?'' Stephanie asked back.

Jesse hopped off the sofa and threw his arms around Stephanie. ''Stephanie, Stephanie!'' he said. ''My favorite niece in the whole world!'' He gave her a too tight hug.

''Did you understand it?'' he asked.

Stephanie laughed again. ''Of course I did! It was a great book. It's a real classic, you know.''

Jesse rubbed his hands together. He peered through the attic window to check that Becky was still outside playing with the boys. Then he raced back to the sofa and patted the space next to him. Stephanie sat down.

''Okay, Steph,'' he began, ''how would you

like to do a great big favor for your absolutely most favorite uncle in the whole wide world?"

Stephanie gave him a suspicious look. "Actually, Uncle Morty on Dad's side is my favorite uncle," she teased.

Jesse ruffled her hair. "Ha, ha, ha," he said. "But seriously, Steph. I need your help. Big time."

"What's up?" Stephanie asked.

Jesse took a deep breath. "It's this book discussion group that Becky and I joined," he told her. "Every two weeks we read a book and then meet at someone's house to discuss it."

"Is it fun?" Stephanie asked.

"Not to me," Jesse replied. "I can't believe people actually do this because they *want* to. I mean, Becky *really* likes the idea."

"Don't you?" Stephanie asked.

Jesse made a disgusted face. "To tell you the truth, I wanted to stop going. But Becky complained that we never do anything like this as a couple, so I agreed to go along with her."

"I think it sounds like a good idea," Stephanie told him.

"Well, never mind that," Jesse said. "The point is that we're supposed to read *The Tale of the*

Willow Tree by Wednesday night, and I can't get past page three!"

"That is a problem," Stephanie agreed.

Jesse ran his fingers through his dark hair. "Last time, we were supposed to read *The Catcher in the Rye*. I just couldn't get into it. But it was my turn to talk about the book. I said I thought it was about baseball, and it turns out that book has *nothing* to do with baseball! Becky was furious with me."

"I guess the title fooled you, huh?" Stephanie asked.

"Right. Anyway, I promised Becky I wouldn't goof off again. I promised her I would read all of the next book. But this story is so boring that I keep falling asleep," Jesse said.

"Really, Uncle Jesse, once you get into it, it's really a very good story, and—" Stephanie tried to say.

"Yeah, yeah, yeah," Jesse interrupted. "So are you going to help me, or what?"

"How can I help you?" Stephanie asked.

"Tell me what it's about so I don't have to read it," Jesse said. "Please? Please? I'll do anything you want in return! Anything!"

Stephanie rested her chin in her hand. *Hmmm. This sounds like the kind of deal I'm looking for.*

She gave Jesse a big smile. "Will you drive me anywhere I need to go for one whole week?" she asked.

"Like where?" Jesse replied.

"To the movies, to a museum, whatever. Tonight, for instance, Darcy and I need a ride to the carnival," Stephanie told him.

Jesse nodded. "No problem!" he exclaimed. "If you tell me about this book . . . I'll drive you to France if you want!"

Stephanie and Jesse shook hands. "It's a deal," Stephanie said. "Then I'll meet you downstairs at seven o'clock. I want to get to the carnival early, to make sure we get right in to Esther's Tent of Wonder."

At seven o'clock on the dot Stephanie and Jesse met at the car. They picked up Darcy at her house. Then Jesse dropped them both off at the carnival. Stephanie and Darcy hurried to Esther's Tent of Wonder and took their place on line.

"Yikes! It's a good thing we got here early," Stephanie said. She gazed behind her. A huge, long line was forming.

"Yeah, I'm glad we're next to go in," Darcy said. "We want to catch Esther while she's still fresh."

"Right. Hey, check this out," Stephanie whispered in Darcy's ear. She pulled a small tape recorder from her jacket pocket and showed it to Darcy.

"What's that for?" Darcy asked.

Stephanie beamed. "I borrowed it from Becky. It's for my article for the paper. I finally found the perfect topic," she explained. "I'm going to expose Esther the Fortune-teller!"

Darcy's mouth opened in surprise. "You're kidding!" she exclaimed.

"Nope. I'm going to tape all her predictions," Stephanie said. "Then, when they don't come true, I'll write a story about how people go overboard believing in phony fortunes, and how dangerous that can be."

Darcy grinned. "Wow . . . just like on TV!"

Stephanie smiled. "I bet it makes the front page of the *Scribe*. But the best part is, it should convince Allie to stop believing in fake fortune-tellers and psychics."

It was their turn to enter the tent. Stephanie

marched up to Esther's table. Esther glanced up at her.

"Stephanie!" she exclaimed with a big smile. "I knew you'd be back!"

Stephanie's mouth dropped open. Her heart nearly skipped a beat.

How did Esther know my name?

CHAPTER
6

♦ ◀ ◢ ♦

Stephanie stared at Esther and then at Darcy. Darcy seemed as surprised as Stephanie.

"Uh, hi," Stephanie answered in a small voice.

Wait a minute, she told herself. *Allie or Darcy must have mentioned my name when we were here last night. Sure, that's it!* She smiled to herself. *Sorry, Esther . . . you can't trick me that easily!*

"You seem happy today," Esther told her.

"Oh, I am happy—now," Stephanie replied.

She and Darcy sat at the table. Stephanie reached into her pocket and pulled out seventy-five cents. She slapped it down in front of Esther and held out her palm. "I'd like the works," she said. "Special cards, palm reading, crystal ball . . . everything!"

Esther shrugged. "Okay, but I thought you didn't believe in fortune-telling," she said.

"Well, I changed my mind," Stephanie fibbed. "I saw some of your predictions come true for my friends."

"Really? Great." Esther placed Stephanie's money in her skirt pocket and then took Stephanie's left hand. She swept her eyes over it, front and back.

Stephanie shoved her right hand into her jacket pocket. She felt the tape recorder and pressed the record button.

"So, does my palm say anything juicy?" Stephanie asked.

Esther studied Stephanie's palm. She closed her eyes and was silent a moment. "Oh, *this* is interesting," she finally said. "I see you come from a large family."

Stephanie pulled her palm away from Esther and studied it herself. "Where?" she demanded. "Where does it say that?"

Esther pointed to a crease on Stephanie's palm. "This is your heritage—or family—line. See how many little lines branch off from it?" she asked.

"I guess," Stephanie said. She glanced at Darcy. Darcy's face wore a stunned expression.

"Wow, Steph," Darcy whispered. "How did she know that?"

"It's probably just another lucky guess," Stephanie whispered back.

Stephanie cleared her throat. "Well, enough palm-reading," she told Esther. "How about a more serious fortune, please?" She tapped the hidden recorder to make sure it was working.

Esther shuffled her fortune-telling cards. She held the pack out to Stephanie. "Choose three cards, please," she said.

Stephanie pulled out the cards.

"Now turn them over," Esther told her. Stephanie turned the cards faceup. The first card showed a woman in a bright green dress surrounded by gold coins. The second card showed two hearts joined together. The third card showed a strange-looking young man with a happy smile on his face. Esther tapped the first card—the one showing the woman.

"I thought there was an air of fortune around you!" Esther exclaimed. "This card shows that you will soon come into money."

"Really? How much money? A little bit or a lot?" Stephanie asked.

Esther shook her head. "I don't know exactly how much," she said. "I just see that you'll come into *some* money."

"Well, I guess coming into money is always a good fortune," Stephanie replied.

And it's an easy prediction to check, she thought. *I'll either get some money or I won't!*

"What do you see in the next card?" Stephanie asked.

Esther pointed to the card with the two connected hearts. "I think you'll like this card," she remarked. "This usually means romance."

"Romance is good," Darcy said. She nudged Stephanie. "I really hope that prediction comes true!" she joked.

"The hearts on the card are a symbol of two-way love," Esther went on. "It means that both people share love and affection equally." She smiled at Stephanie. "This card can be very, very good. And I do think there's a boy . . . a special boy . . . who likes you a lot. No—he *loves* you," Esther added. "And I think he will tell you how he feels sooner rather than later."

Stephanie stared at the hearts card. For a moment she forgot all about the tape recorder in her pocket. *Some boy loves me? Wow!* she thought.

"Well, who is he?" she asked. "Do I know him already, or is it someone totally new, or—?"

Esther held up a hand, signaling Stephanie to be silent. Esther closed her eyes, and Stephanie held her breath. Darcy sat on the edge of her seat, waiting for Esther to speak again.

"I see the letter *N*," Esther finally said.

"The letter *N*?" Stephanie asked.

"Neil Lippman!" Darcy squealed. "You know, that guy in your social studies class! I *know* he likes you, Steph!"

Stephanie made a face. "Oh, yuck!" she said. "I hope *not!*" She glanced at Esther. "Is it Neil Lippman?" she asked.

Esther shrugged. "I can't tell you that. I just see an *N*. Besides, you forget that the hearts are joined—with love on *both* sides."

"That's right," Stephanie murmured. "And I definitely *don't* love Neil Lippman." Stephanie stared at Esther. "What about the rest of the letters in this guy's name?" she asked.

"I see nothing else," Esther said.

"Not even his last initial?" Stephanie prodded.

"I'm sorry, Stephanie, but all I see is an *N*," Esther replied.

Stephanie felt a wave of disappointment. *Wait a minute*, she told herself. *Now I'm getting carried away!*

Stephanie reached into her pocket and switched off the tape recorder. "No offense, Esther, but one letter isn't a whole lot of information," she said.

"I think I told you something more useful than that," Esther said.

"Well, I don't," Stephanie said. "I don't think you told me anything more than—than a fortune cookie I once got. It said that someday I'll be famous and my lucky number is seven." She turned to Darcy. "Come on, Darce. Let's go home."

Stephanie and Darcy both stood up, getting ready to leave.

"Stephanie, wait," Esther said. "Your lucky number isn't seven. It's four!"

"That was totally weird, don't you think?" Stephanie asked as she and Darcy hurried through the arcade. They were supposed to meet

Uncle Jesse on the other side of the carnival in a few minutes.

"What?" Darcy asked.

"Well, the way I started to want to believe Esther's predictions," Stephanie said. "I mean, the one about some guy being in love with me!"

Darcy nodded. "I got pretty caught up in that, too," she admitted.

"Yeah," Stephanie said thoughtfully. "I guess now I can see how Allie might get so carried away. I mean, it would be great if that *N* guy was real."

Stephanie sighed. "Anyway, I think I have enough information now to start my article. But I'd better wait a few days to see if Esther's predictions come true," Stephanie said. "Then if they don't, I can expose her as a phony."

Darcy frowned. "What if her predictions come true?" she asked.

"I don't think they will. Think about it," Stephanie told her. "The predictions that came true for you and Allie were really only lucky guesses—things that could happen to anyone. Everybody loses something or wins money sometime."

"I see your point," Darcy said.

"Sure. She has no real information at all,"

Stephanie went on. "She probably just makes up this stuff as she goes along."

They reached the meeting place, and Stephanie searched for Uncle Jesse. He wasn't there yet.

Darcy shook her head. "Wait a minute, Steph," she said. "How did she know that you have a big family?"

Stephanie frowned. "I don't know. Maybe something about me gave it away," she replied.

"Maybe," Darcy said.

"Anyway, suppose she told me that I was an animal lover or an athlete—like she told you and Allie. She wouldn't have been *wrong*," Stephanie added. "I mean, I like animals, and I'm also a pretty good athlete."

"That's true," Darcy agreed.

"Sure. A lot of what she says could be true for *anybody*," Stephanie said.

She chuckled. "Like I'm really going to inherit a lot of money and fall in love with some guy named Ned! Get real, Darcy."

Darcy chuckled, too. "Yeah, I guess it *does* sound pretty silly when you put it that way."

"Of course it does!" Stephanie patted the pocket holding her tape recorder. "I'm just glad I got this meeting on tape. Now I can't wait to start my article. Just think, Darce—if I can prove that Esther's predictions aren't real, then Allie won't cut school. She might even stop reading horoscope books all the time."

"And go to the movies with us again, and eat whatever she wants!" Darcy giggled. "But really, I can't wait to have Allie back to normal," she added.

"Yeah. That would be great," Stephanie said.

A few more minutes passed. Stephanie glanced at her watch. "I wonder where Uncle Jesse is?" she mumbled.

"Hey, look, Steph," Darcy said. "Isn't that your favorite arcade game—the Clown Squirt Race?"

"Where?" Stephanie asked.

"A few booths down." Darcy pointed in the opposite direction.

"Oh, yeah, I see it!" Stephanie replied. "I'm so great at that game! Let's go play, Darce."

Stephanie and Darcy hurried to the booth. They each grabbed a water gun. Six more people lined up behind the remaining squirt guns. The starting bell rang.

Stephanie aimed her water gun at the clown's mouth and pulled the trigger. A steady stream of water shot out, right into the clown's mouth.

Above the clown's head, a bright blue balloon grew as Stephanie squirted in more and more water.

Darcy glanced over at her. "Keep it up, Steph!" she shouted. "You're doing great!"

Darcy's balloon flopped over, but Stephanie's balloon got bigger and bigger.

Ka-boom! It exploded.

"Clown number four is the winner!" the man who ran the booth announced.

Stephanie slapped Darcy a high five. "All right!" she cheered.

"Wait a minute!" Darcy stared at Stephanie. "Did he just say clown number *four?*" Darcy took a deep breath. "Esther said four is your lucky number!"

Stephanie blinked. "Wow. That's a weird coincidence."

"Ready to claim your prize?" the man asked.

"Sure, what do I win?" Stephanie asked. "A stuffed turtle? A goldfish?"

"Nope." The man reached into his pocket. He pulled out a twenty-dollar bill and handed it to Stephanie.

Stephanie gaped at the money. "I won . . . *twenty dollars?*"

Darcy gasped. "Stephanie! You've come into money! Just like Esther said!"

Stephanie shoved the bill deep into her pocket. "That's crazy, Darce. I won the money because I'm really good at this game."

"Well, you are good at it, but you don't always win first prize, do you?" Darcy asked.

"I guess not," Stephanie admitted. "Darcy, this can't have anything to do with Esther's prediction, can it?"

Darcy shrugged. "I don't know, Steph. I really don't know."

Stephanie stared at Darcy.

This can't be happening, she told herself. *Esther's predictions can't be true!*

Stephanie and Darcy walked slowly away from the game arcade. Stephanie spotted something gleaming on the ground. She stooped over.

"Look—I just found a quarter! More money!" Stephanie cried. She felt a wave of relief. "See? That could fit Esther's prediction, too," she said. She handed Darcy the quarter.

"I'm so confused!" Darcy said.

"I know. It is confusing," Stephanie agreed. "Which proves one thing."

"What's that?" Darcy asked.

"It's really important that I write that article. I'm more convinced than ever—fortune-tellers are more than fakes. They're dangerous. And that makes me worry about Allie."

"It makes me worry, too," Darcy agreed.

"Well, I won't just sit around feeling worried about our best friend," Stephanie declared. "I'm going to do something about it!"

CHAPTER
7

◆ ◀ ◢ ◆

Sunday afternoon, Stephanie sat in front of the computer. She was in her father's office on the second floor of their house. Her fingers flew over the keys as she began typing her article for the *Scribe*. She couldn't believe how great it was turning out. Telling the truth about fortune-tellers was probably her best story idea ever.

Stephanie finished typing and printed the article. Then she called Darcy.

"Hi, Steph. What's up?" Darcy said when she answered the phone.

"I wrote my article!" Stephanie announced.

"Great," Darcy replied.

"I really want to show it to you. Can you meet me at the mall? Uncle Jesse is driving me there in a little while. I want to spend my carnival winnings on new CDs at Beats."

"Oh, I'd love to, but I can't," Darcy said. "I'm going food shopping with my mom soon."

"Too bad," Stephanie said. "You're going to love the angle I came up with. I wrote the story as if I was following Allie around."

"How'd you do that?" Darcy asked.

"Well, first I show how Allie was lured into the world of fortune-telling in the first place. Then I show how Allie gets so involved in fortunes and horoscopes that she starts spending all her money on rocks and crystals and stuff."

"Yeah. That's pretty interesting," Darcy said.

"And it winds up with Allie not making a move without calling The Psychic Hot Line," Stephanie went on.

"Sounds great. Why don't you read it to me?" Darcy suggested.

"Sure." Stephanie read the article into the phone.

Darcy listened on the other end of the line until Stephanie finished reading.

"So?" Stephanie asked. "What do you think?"

Darcy cleared her throat. "Well . . ."

"Come on, Darce! Give it to me straight!" Stephanie ordered.

"Well, there's one little problem," Darcy said.

"What is it?" Stephanie asked.

"You'd better change Allie's name in the article," Darcy said. "She won't like everyone knowing that she's obsessed with fortune-tellers—or that she calls The Psychic Hot Line five times a day."

Stephanie nodded. "Good idea," she said. "I'm glad you warned me. So if I do that, then do you think the article is okay?"

"Actually, it's pretty good," Darcy admitted.

"Thanks! It was really exciting writing it. In fact, I think I'm going to make it a two-part article," Stephanie said.

"What will the second part be about?" Darcy asked.

"Well, I plan to show Allie finding out that Esther's predictions are fake," Stephanie explained. "And that fortune-tellers are ordinary people in flashy costumes who can't predict a rainstorm."

"That would be great!" Darcy said.

"Yeah. But it means I have to go back to see Esther again," Stephanie said.

"I guess so," Darcy said.

"I'll have to play the tape I made of our last visit," Stephanie explained. "Then I'll force her to explain why I never met my dream guy with the letter *N*."

"That would be fantastic," Darcy agreed. "Stephanie, I have to admit—you make a great investigative journalist. You have no shame at all!"

Stephanie grinned. "Thanks! Actually, I think I might add something to part one," she told Darcy. "I think I should warn people that following the advice of horoscopes and fortunes can be dangerous stuff. It could lead you into big trouble."

"Speaking of big trouble, tomorrow is Monday," Darcy said.

"Right." Stephanie was silent a minute. "I'm really worried about Allie. She's not still planning to cut, is she?" Stephanie asked.

Darcy sighed. "Yeah. I talked to her right before you called. She said she won't change her mind."

Stephanie shook her head. "I can't believe that she won't listen to us about it."

"Well, maybe you should call her and read her your article," Darcy said. "It might change her mind."

"Are you kidding? Allie is so stubborn. She'd never even listen to me read it," Stephanie pointed out.

"I guess you're right," Darcy said. "Anyway, have fun at the mall. I'll see you tomorrow morning."

"Right. Meet me at our usual place—the pay phone by the gym," Stephanie said.

"Right. I'll be there," Darcy replied.

Stephanie hung up the phone, then shouted upstairs. "Uncle Jesse! I'm ready to go!"

A minute later, Jesse rushed down the stairs. He was grinning, and he waved his car keys above his head. "The Jesse Express is heading out. Destination: the mall!"

"You're going *out?*" a voice called from the kitchen.

Jesse stopped in his tracks. He turned to see Becky standing in the kitchen doorway.

"Oh! Hi, honey! I didn't know you were there," Jesse said.

Becky folded her arms across her chest. "Jesse, how can you go to the mall now? I mean, I haven't seen you crack open *The Tale of the Willow Tree* all week! Our discussion group meets in only three days."

Jesse waved his hand, as if he wasn't worried about a thing. "Oh, *that!*" he said. "Don't worry, Beck. I'm on top of it."

"Oh, really?" Becky asked. "You mean, you finished reading the book?"

Jesse swallowed hard. "Well, not exactly *finished . . .*" he began.

Becky's eyes narrowed.

"I'm *almost* finished," he said, edging to the door. "I'm at the part where, you know, um . . ."

Stephanie stepped up close behind him and whispered, "Where the little boy meets the old gentleman under the tree."

"Uh, where the little boy meets the old gentleman," Jesse called out. "Under the willow tree."

Becky's eyes widened. "Wow, Jess, I'm impressed! You *are* reading it!" She blew him a kiss. "I'm sorry I doubted you, sweetie." She turned and walked back into the kitchen.

When Becky was gone, Jesse breathed a huge sigh of relief. "That was too close!" he exclaimed. "Steph, you have to tell me the rest of the plot—and fast!"

Stephanie pushed Jesse out the door. "Okay, okay . . . but in the car," she said. "On the way to the mall."

Stephanie searched every aisle at Beats. She plowed through racks and racks of CDs. She didn't see a single one that interested her.

She was about to give up when a deep voice called to her.

"Can I help you with something?"

Stephanie was about to say, "No, thanks." Then she spotted the salesboy who had spoken to her. He was tall and thin, with curly brown hair. His bright smile set off deep blue eyes and dimpled cheeks.

What a cute guy! Stephanie thought.

"Uh, maybe you can help me," she said as he walked up to her. "I was looking for some new CDs but I can't find anything special."

The salesboy grinned. "You didn't look in the right place! We just got in some great new music," he said. "Follow me."

He hurried across the store. Stephanie followed him up to a rack of CDs that she hadn't noticed before. The rack was labeled Alternative Rock.

"These are brand-new," the salesboy said. "I just put them on display this morning. They are *definitely* different."

Stephanie managed a smile. She wasn't exactly a big fan of alternative rock. But she flipped through the rack and pretended to be interested.

"Oh, sure—Purple Sky—I've heard of them," she said, reading the back of the CD case.

"If you like them, you'll love this new CD from The Toners," the salesboy said. "I listen to their old stuff all the time. They're on tour in California right now, you know."

Stephanie pretended to know all about The Toners. "Yeah, these guys are hot," she said. Then she glanced at the price of the CD. It was a new release, so it cost more than she wanted to spend.

"I can give you a special price," the salesboy said.

Stephanie felt her face turn red. "Wow— thanks!" she told him.

The boy grinned. "Just don't tell my manager. I'm not really supposed to discount the new stuff yet," he told her.

Stephanie ran her fingers through her hair. *I hope I look okay*, she thought. She smiled up at the boy.

"Thanks! Okay, I'll take this one," she said.

"Great! Come on up to the cash register," he said.

Stephanie followed him back to the front of the store. She felt as if she were floating on air. This guy was being unbelievably nice.

"You know, I never noticed you here before," Stephanie said. "When did you start working here?"

"Two weeks ago," he told her. He rang up the CD.

Stephanie handed him her money and watched as he placed the CD in a shopping bag.

"Are you on our mailing list yet?" he asked.

"No." Stephanie shook her head.

He handed her a form to fill out. "You can get lots of special prices if you're on the list," he explained. "And we'll let you know when our big sales are coming up."

Stephanie filled out the form. She sneaked a few glances in his direction. "All done," she said when she was finished. She handed him the form. "Well, uh, it was nice meeting you," she said. "Thanks for the help."

"No problem. Oh, hey, if you're still hanging around the mall around six-thirty, why don't you come back?" he suggested. "We'll be playing the Toners' new boxed set."

Stephanie's heart pounded. *He wants me to come back!* she thought.

She glanced at her watch. It was only four-thirty. She groaned. Uncle Jesse would never agree to hang around the mall for another two hours.

"That sounds cool, but I can't hang out that late," Stephanie said. "My ride has to leave soon."

The boy shrugged. "Too bad. But okay," he said.

Just then another salesboy appeared behind the register. "Hey, Nathaniel," he called. "Mark needs you in the stockroom."

"I've got to run. Mark's the store manager," the boy explained to Stephanie. He glanced at the form Stephanie had just handed him. "So, maybe I'll catch you later—Stephanie Tanner."

"Yeah, um, later!" Stephanie called as he disappeared into the stockroom.

Later, she thought dreamily as she hurried to meet Uncle Jesse. She couldn't get the boy's face out of her mind. She walked through the mall, seeing only his deep blue eyes and that adorable smile.

She wondered how old he was. Fifteen? Sixteen? She wondered where he went to school.

Jesse was already waiting in the car in front of the mall entrance. Stephanie hopped into the front seat and snapped on her seat belt. She couldn't wait to get home and call Allie and Darcy to tell them the big news. The most amazing guy had just asked her for a date!

CHAPTER
8

◆ ◀ ◼ ◆

Stephanie raced through the kitchen and into the living room. She dropped her Beat shopping bag on the sofa and headed straight for the phone. Before she could dial, D.J. appeared on the stairs, followed by four people Stephanie had never seen before.

"Hey, D.J.," Stephanie called. "What's going on?"

D.J. stacked a pile of textbooks on the coffee table and sat down wearily on the sofa. Her friends sat down, too. "Hi, Steph," D.J. said. "This is my study group. We're working on a project for my psychology class. Everyone, this is my sister Stephanie. She was just leaving."

71

Stephanie rolled her eyes. She grabbed her shopping bag off the couch. "Well, I don't want to get in your way. I'll just use the phone in the kitchen," she said.

Nobody answered. In the kitchen, Stephanie dialed Darcy's house, but the line was busy. And nobody was home at Allie's, either.

It figures! Stephanie groaned. *I meet the guy of my dreams, and nobody is around to tell about it!*

Stephanie hung up the phone. The kitchen door swung open, and one of the boys from D.J.'s study group burst into the room. He had dark hair and dark eyes. He was cute, Stephanie noticed. Nearly as cute as the salesboy.

Today must be my day to run into cute guys, Stephanie thought.

"Excuse me," he said, "but, um, could I get a glass for a soda?"

"Sure." Stephanie pulled a glass from the kitchen cabinet and showed him where they kept the sodas in the refrigerator. She noticed that he wore a T-shirt that said THE TONERS.

"Hey, do you like The Toners?" she asked.

The boy's face lit up. "Like them? I love them! How did you guess?"

"Uh, it wasn't hard," Stephanie said. She pointed to his T-shirt.

"Oh, right!" He laughed. "You know, not many people like their music."

Stephanie pulled the CD from the shopping bag. "I just bought their latest CD," she said.

"Wow!" he exclaimed. "I didn't know it was even out yet!"

"Oh, yeah," Stephanie said. "It just came out today. They're touring California, you know."

The boy's eyes widened. "No way!" he said. "Man, I would love to see them in concert."

Stephanie nodded, then dropped the CD back in the bag. She headed for the stairs. She could try calling Darcy and Allie from the phone in her dad's office upstairs.

"Hey, Stephanie, wait!" the boy called after her. "Can I, um, ask you something?"

Stephanie shrugged. "Sure. What's up?"

"I, uh, wanted to ask you a question," the guy said. "Um, I wanted to ask about—"

At that moment, D.J. burst through the kitchen door. "Hey, Jake!" she said. "Come on! We need you in here."

Jake stopped talking. He grabbed his glass of cola. "Oh, sure, D.J.," he said. "Um, see you

73

later, Stephanie!" He followed D.J. back into the living room.

Stephanie stared after him. What was *that* all about? she wondered. She bent over to pick up her shopping bag. She could hardly wait to get upstairs and listen to the CD.

And I would never have bought it if Nathaniel hadn't told me—She suddenly froze.

Nathaniel! The other salesboy had called her salesclerk *Nathaniel*— with an *N!*

Stephanie felt a shiver run down her spine.

Nathaniel . . .

Stephanie's jaw dropped. She collapsed onto a chair in shock.

I just met an incredibly cute guy. And he was interested in me. And his name begins with the letter N!

She swallowed hard.

Did this mean what she thought it meant? Was Esther right? Was Nathaniel her dream guy?

Stephanie's head was swimming with confusion. She didn't know *what* to believe!

"Pssst! Steph!" a voice called.

Stephanie's heart skipped a beat. "Who's that?" she called. She jumped up and gazed

74

around the kitchen. "Whoever you are, where are you?" she asked.

"Over here, Stephanie! Behind the basement door!"

"Uncle Jesse!" Stephanie recognized his voice. She rushed over to the basement door and yanked it open. Jesse grabbed her arm and pulled her onto the landing.

"Uncle Jesse!" she exclaimed. "You scared me!"

Jesse put a finger to his lips. "Shhh," he whispered. He opened the door again and peered into the kitchen.

"Did you see Becky out there?" he asked.

"No, I haven't seen her at all," Stephanie said.

Jesse sighed with relief. "Good!" he said. "You have to help me . . . and fast. Becky's been following me around all day, asking me a million questions about *The Tale of the Willow Tree!* I'm running out of excuses. You have to tell me the rest of the story before it's too late!"

"Uncle Jesse, why don't you just read the end of the book?" Stephanie asked. "It really is a great story."

Jesse stared at her. "Are you trying to back out of our deal?" he asked.

"No way!" Stephanie replied. "It's just that I think you should read the book. Once you get into it, you'll really like it."

Jesse rolled his eyes. "You sound just like—"

The basement door flew open.

"Aha!" Becky exclaimed. "There you are, Jesse!"

Jesse gulped. "Hi, Becky," he said. "Were you looking for me?"

Becky folded her arms across her chest. "Only for the past half hour!" she replied. "Where have you been? The boys want you to help them set up their trains."

Jesse motioned toward the basement, where the musical equipment for his rock band was all set up. "I've been rehearsing a little," he said.

"Well, can you take a break to help the boys?" Becky asked.

"Sure!" Jesse said. He glanced at Stephanie. "I guess we'll, um, talk about your history homework a little later, Steph. If that's okay with you."

"Oh, right, my history homework," Stephanie said.

"You asked Jesse to help with history?" Becky said in amazement. "He's terrible at history."

"I just needed someone to quiz me on a chapter," Stephanie fibbed.

"I'd be glad to do that," Becky told her.

"No, no, honey, we're all done," Jesse said. "Now I need you to help me upstairs with the trains, okay?"

"Well, sure," Becky said. She and Jesse headed toward the kitchen stairs to go up to the attic apartment.

Stephanie sighed and picked up her shopping bag again. *Finally!* she thought. She raced up to her room and slipped the new CD into her CD player.

Actually, the music wasn't that bad, she realized. And if Nathaniel liked it, she could learn to like it, too!

CHAPTER
9

◆ ◀ ◾ ◆

Stephanie glanced at her watch. It was still very early in the morning.

Good, she told herself. *There's plenty of time to get to Allie's house and change her mind about cutting school today.*

She doubled her speed as she ran down the street.

"Stephanie!" someone called.

Stephanie glanced up in surprise. "Darcy! What are you doing here?" she asked. She skidded to a stop on the sidewalk. Darcy crossed the street and hurried over to her.

"The same as you, I bet." Darcy grinned. "Are you going to Allie's?"

"Yes," Stephanie said. "I figured if I got there early enough, I could convince her not to cut today. And we could still make it to school on time."

"That's what I thought, too," Darcy said. "Anyway, it's worth a try."

Darcy fell into step beside Stephanie. They hurried together the rest of the way to Allie's house.

Stephanie shook her head. "I can't believe she's trying to go through with this. She could get in so much trouble! I mean, what if the school calls her house?"

"She said she was going to pretend she's her own mother on the phone," Darcy told her.

"You're kidding!" Stephanie exclaimed.

"Nope. I told her it was a dumb idea," Darcy said. "But Allie isn't listening to me these days. She only listens to Anna, her pal from The Psychic Hot Line."

"I know," Stephanie said. "I can't believe she listens to a total stranger, but not her best friends."

"It's driving me crazy," Darcy admitted. "It's like I can't talk to Allie anymore. I wish we could get her interested in something else. Like boys, or even homework, or maybe—"

"Hey—I almost forgot!" Stephanie interrupted. "Speaking of boys, I have incredible news."

"Really? What?" Darcy asked.

Stephanie broke into a huge grin. "I'm in love!" she announced.

"What? With who?" Darcy demanded.

"Well, he works at Beats," Stephanie began. "His name is Nathaniel, and he's totally, completely gorgeous! I went in yesterday to buy a new CD with my carnival money and—"

"Wait a second!" Darcy interrupted. "Stephanie, did you say *Nathaniel?*"

Stephanie nodded. *Here it comes*, she thought.

"Nathaniel . . . as with the initial *N?*" Darcy stared.

"It's true." Stephanie sighed.

"Then it's the guy Esther was talking about!" Darcy shouted. "It happened!"

"I knew you would say that," Stephanie said. "And I admit . . . I thought about the same thing. But then I realized, it could be just another coincidence. I don't even know if he *really* likes me.

I mean, he just asked me to meet him back at the store and I—"

"He asked you for a *date?*" Darcy squealed.

"No, not exactly," Stephanie told her. "He just said that if I happened to stay at the mall, I should come back to hear a new CD in the store."

"Sounds to me like he's really interested in you," Darcy said.

"I hope so. Oh, Darcy, I just have to get back to that store to see Nathaniel again!" Stephanie told her.

Darcy grinned. "Don't worry, Steph. You'll see him. Esther said so!"

Stephanie groaned. "Esther has nothing to do with this," she insisted.

Just a coincidence, she told herself.

Or was it?

They turned the corner. Allie's house was right in front of them. "I don't see any cars in the driveway," Stephanie whispered. "Her parents must have gone to work already."

"Then why are we whispering?" Darcy asked. She giggled.

Stephanie giggled back, and they walked up to the front door.

"Hey, you guys! Over here!" Allie called to them.

Stephanie and Darcy whirled around. Allie crawled out from under the hedge at the side of the house.

"Allie! What are you doing there?" Stephanie asked.

"Hiding!" Allie said. "I was waiting in the bushes until my parents left for work," she explained. She straightened up and rubbed a big red welt on her leg.

Stephanie stared at it. "What's that?" she asked.

Allie took a deep breath. "I got stung by a bee!" she wailed.

"Are you okay?" Stephanie asked.

"I think so. It only swelled a little bit," Allie said.

"You need to put some ointment on that," Darcy told her.

"You're right. Let's go in my house," Allie replied. She led them to the back door and unlocked it with her key. "What are you guys doing here, anyway?" she asked.

Stephanie and Darcy exchanged guilty looks.

"Uh, we thought we could talk you out of cutting school," Stephanie admitted.

"Please, Al—don't do it," Darcy added. "You could get in big trouble. Come with us, okay?"

"No way!" Allie declared. "You know I have to avoid bad luck today."

"Uh—isn't it bad luck to get stung by a bee when you're hiding?" Stephanie asked.

Allie looked annoyed. "It's not as bad as what would happen at school," she insisted.

"Well, if you're staying here, we're staying with you," Stephanie told her.

"Right," Darcy agreed.

"But I don't want to get you guys in trouble," Allie told them.

"Too bad. We're staying." Stephanie tossed her backpack on a kitchen chair. Darcy did the same. "Lead us to the ointment!" Stephanie said.

Allie led them into the bathroom. She searched through the medicine cabinet. "No ointment," she muttered.

"Try the linen closet," Darcy suggested. "My mom keeps stuff like that on a top shelf of our closet."

"Good idea," Allie said. She went into the

hallway and opened the linen closet door. "Hey! There is some, way up on the top shelf."

"I guess all mothers think alike," Darcy joked.

"Where's your step stool?" Stephanie asked.

"I don't need one," Allie replied. She placed one foot on the bottom shelf and hoisted herself up. "I do this all the time," she said. She balanced as she reached up to the top shelf. She snatched up the tube of ointment.

"You know, that shelf looks kind of—" Darcy began.

Craaash!

The bottom shelf collapsed. Allie let out a squawk as she tumbled to the floor.

"Allie!" Stephanie cried. She rushed to her side. "Are you okay?"

Allie sat up, rubbing her ankle. "Oh! My foot hurts!"

"I think you twisted it," Stephanie said.

Darcy stooped down and examined Allie's ankle. "I've done that playing tennis. You need to put some ice on this," she told her.

Darcy and Stephanie helped Allie hop into the kitchen. They rubbed ointment on her bee sting, then pulled an ice pack from the freezer and set it on her ankle.

"My ankle feels better already," Allie said.

"Poor Allie!" Stephanie shook her head.

Darcy laughed. "Yeah, and the crazy thing is, you stayed home so you *wouldn't* have any bad luck."

"Really. If you went to school today, none of this would have happened," Stephanie added.

"No. You guys have it all backward," Allie said. "If you left me home alone, this would never have happened."

"How do you figure that?" Stephanie asked.

"Yeah," Darcy added. "Esther said to beware of groups of people. There's no group here."

Allie gave an impatient sigh. "The three of us are a group," she pointed out. "You guys made me have bad luck."

Stephanie and Darcy exchanged looks of surprise. "Oops," Darcy said.

"I refuse to believe that," Stephanie said. "No way."

"Well, it doesn't matter now," Allie said. She took the ice pack off her ankle and stood up. "My foot feels okay." She lifted her backpack off the kitchen chair. "If you're going to hang around me all day, we might as well go to school."

"Yay!" Stephanie cheered. She glanced at her watch. "If we really hurry, we won't even be late!"

Stephanie wondered about fortunes and fortune-tellers the rest of the day at school. She was still wondering about them when she entered her house that afternoon. She had barely put down her backpack when Michelle handed her a slip of paper.

"Some guy named Nathaniel called you," Michelle told her. "He left his phone number so you can call him at work."

Stephanie's jaw fell open. "Nathaniel?" she exclaimed. "Are you sure?"

"Yup." Michelle nodded.

Stephanie stared at the piece of paper in her hand. "What else did he say? Tell me everything," Stephanie demanded.

"I did tell you everything!" Michelle replied.

Stephanie rushed to pick up the phone.

"Are you calling him back?" Michelle asked.

"Not yet. First I have to call Darcy." Stephanie dialed, and Darcy picked up on the first ring.

"What's up?" Darcy asked.

"Big news!" Stephanie exclaimed. "Guess who

called me—Nathaniel! He left a message for me to call him back."

"Did you?" Darcy asked.

"Not yet," Stephanie said. "I called you first!"

The front doorbell rang. "Hang on, Darce," Stephanie said. She carried the cordless phone to the door. She opened it. "Oh!" she said. "Hi, Jake."

Jake smiled as he stepped inside the house. "Hey, Stephanie, I'm really glad you're here," he said. "There's something I want to ask you. See, I—"

"Hey, Jake!" D.J. called. She bounded down the stairs and stopped next to Stephanie in the doorway. "What are you doing here?"

Stephanie noticed that Jake seemed suddenly uncomfortable. His face flushed, and he shifted from one foot to the other.

"Uh, hi, D.J.!" he said. "I, um, came for my notebook. I think I left it here last night."

"You did," D.J. said. "I put it on this table with my own books." D.J. picked up a green notebook and handed it to Jake.

"Oh. Well, then, thanks," Jake said. He glanced at Stephanie for a moment and then looked back at D.J. "Well, I guess I better get going. Bye, Stephanie. See you in class tomorrow, D.J."

Jake left, and D.J. closed the door behind him. She turned and gazed thoughtfully at Stephanie. "I have a funny feeling," D.J. said. "I think Jake likes you, Steph."

"Me?" Stephanie blinked in surprise. "What makes you say that?"

"Well, for one thing, he could have called to ask me to bring his notebook to class tomorrow," D.J. said. "He didn't have to come over here to get it."

"Maybe he likes *you*," Stephanie said.

"I don't think so," D.J. answered. "Jake is only sixteen," she added. "He skipped a couple of grades, so he's younger than most of the girls in our college class. I know he hasn't gone out with anyone yet because of it."

"So you think he likes me because I'm not too old for him?" Stephanie asked.

"Maybe," D.J. replied. "It could be he was hoping to see you when he came to get his notebook just now."

"I don't know about that," Stephanie said.

"Well, are you interested?" D.J. asked. "I could find out if he likes you, you know."

"I don't know, Deej, I—yikes!" Stephanie exclaimed. "I almost forgot! Darcy's still on the phone!"

D.J. shrugged and headed into the kitchen. Stephanie lifted the phone again. "Darce—are you still there?" she asked.

"Of course I am! But who's Jake?" Darcy asked.

"He's one of D.J.'s friends," Stephanie told her. "D.J. thinks he might like me!"

"I heard her say that. Do you like him?" Darcy asked.

"I don't know. Who can think about Jake when Nathaniel likes me?" Stephanie asked. "I mean, Jake's name doesn't even start with an *N*."

"You'd better call Nathaniel back right now," Darcy told her. "Maybe he wants to say that he's madly in love with you."

Stephanie rolled her eyes. "I'll call you later," she told Darcy. "Good-bye!" She hung up and dialed Beats.

"Hello?" a man's voice asked.

"Um, hello," Stephanie replied. "Can I speak with Nathaniel, please?"

"Nathaniel's gone for the day," the man replied. "Try him tomorrow. He works later then."

"Oh. Okay, thanks," Stephanie said. She pressed the off button and leaned back on the sofa. Tomorrow! She had to wait a whole day before finding out what Nathaniel wanted?

Oh, well. Better late than never, she told herself. She closed her eyes and pictured him again. That adorable smile. The way he said, "Catch you later, Stephanie Tanner."

Stephanie sighed. *Esther . . . even though I still think you're a fake, and I'm sure this is just a coincidence . . . I hope you're right about Nathaniel!*

CHAPTER
10

◆ ◀ ◆ ◆

"Hey, Allie!" Stephanie rushed up to the pay phone. It was early the next morning.

"Shhh!" Allie hissed at her. She turned her back, and Stephanie realized she was talking on the phone.

"Don't bother her," Darcy told Stephanie. "She's been gabbing away forever."

"Who is she talking to?" Stephanie asked.

Darcy sighed. "Anna, her psychic adviser," she said.

Stephanie groaned. "Not Anna again! Allie does everything that crazy woman says. She'd wear all her clothes backward and upside down if Anna said so!"

Allie hung up the phone and turned around. She glared at Stephanie.

"What's wrong?" Stephanie asked her.

"I heard that, Stephanie! You don't have to dump on Anna!" Allie shook her head. "You're acting just like Anna said you would," she added.

"Huh?" Stephanie asked.

"Anna warned me. She said to avoid people spreading bad vibes this morning." Allie lifted her chin. "The bad vibes are coming from you!"

"Hold on, Al," Darcy started to say.

"No, you're just as bad as Stephanie," Allie told Darcy. "I don't want either of you to talk to me for the rest of the day. And don't sit near me at lunch, either." Allie spun on her heel and marched down the hall.

Stephanie and Darcy stared after her in disbelief.

"I don't believe it," Darcy said.

"We have to do something!" Stephanie exclaimed. "Our best friend is totally losing her mind!"

Stephanie worried about Allie all morning. At lunch she could only pick at her chicken salad sandwich. She lifted a copy of the *Scribe* and stared at it blankly. It had just come out that morning, and this was her first chance to check out her article. But she could barely concentrate on what she was reading.

Darcy dropped her backpack on the table and plopped down next to Stephanie. "Front-page article," she said. "Way to go, Steph!"

Stephanie grinned. "Yeah, it is pretty cool, isn't it?" she asked.

"Very cool!" Darcy replied. "But I didn't get to read it yet, either. Do you have an extra copy?"

Stephanie pulled a half-dozen copies from her backpack. "How many do you want?" she asked. "Three? Four?"

"Just one." Darcy chuckled. She took a copy and started to read. Seconds later, another backpack landed on the table. Darcy and Stephanie glanced up.

"Allie!" Stephanie smiled. "Did you see my article?"

Allie's lips were pursed together tightly and her face was red. She waved a copy of the *Scribe* in Stephanie's face.

"How could you do this to me?" she demanded.

Stephanie stopped smiling. "Allie, why are you so mad?"

Allie tossed the newspaper onto the table. "Why do you think I'm mad?"

"I don't know. Because I wrote bad things about Esther?" Stephanie asked.

Allie's face grew even redder. "No, because of what you wrote about *me!* How could you use me like that?"

Darcy scanned the article. "Stephanie, I thought you changed the girl's name in your story," she said.

"I did!" Stephanie insisted.

Allie threw up her hands. "Oh, like everyone in this entire school can't figure out that 'Ellie Tyler' is really your best friend, Allie Taylor! What were you thinking?"

"But . . . but the story isn't about you, exactly," Stephanie said. "It's about exposing the truth behind phony fortune-telling."

Allie stared at her. "Oh, really? Well, ever since this stupid article came out, kids have been teasing me left and right about what a sucker I am!"

Stephanie gulped. "They have?" she asked.

"I can't walk down the hall without hearing a crystal ball joke!" Allie snapped.

"Allie, I'm sorry!" Stephanie exclaimed. "I really didn't mean to—"

"Hey, 'Ellie'!" a boy at the next table called to Allie. "Is it okay for me to sit at this table today? I don't want bad lunchroom karma to ruin my fish sticks!" He burst out laughing, along with his entire group of friends.

Allie clenched her fists. "See?"

"That's not funny!" Stephanie shouted at the boy.

One of the boy's friends tossed a red pen at Allie. "Here, take this!" he called.

Allie made a face. "What's this for?" she asked.

"I'd like my palm *red!*" he shouted back.

The boys hooted and slapped each other high fives. Allie picked up her backpack and glared at Stephanie.

"I'll never forgive you for this, Stephanie!" Allie declared. She grabbed her backpack and stormed away.

"Come back, Allie!" Stephanie called after her. "I'm sorry!"

Allie rushed out of the cafeteria. Stephanie sank into her chair. "I really didn't mean for this to happen," she told Darcy.

"I've never seen Allie so angry before," Darcy said.

"I can't believe she's acting like that," Stephanie said. "Ever since Allie talked to Esther, she's gotten worse and worse," Stephanie grumbled. "In fact, if it wasn't for Esther, none of this would have happened!"

Darcy shook her head. "I don't know, Steph. Allie is the one who got herself hooked on fortunes and psychics. I'll talk to her," she promised. "I'll make her see that you didn't mean to embarrass her. But promise me one thing," she added.

"What's that?" Stephanie asked.

Darcy frowned. "When you write part two of your article, don't use the name Ellie Tyler!"

Stephanie sank lower in her chair. "I promise!"

Stephanie knocked on the front door of Allie's house. She had hurried there right after school. Mrs. Taylor answered the door. "Hello, Stephanie," she said. "I'm sorry, but Allie told me to tell you she's too busy for visitors right now."

Stephanie sighed. "I had a feeling Allie wouldn't see me," she said. Allie hadn't spoken to Stephanie the rest of the day at school. Stephanie had guessed that she probably wouldn't talk to her now, either.

Stephanie reached into her backpack and took out a letter she had written in study hall. It apologized for the article and asked Allie to forgive her.

"Could you give Allie this note?" she asked Allie's mom.

"Of course." Mrs. Taylor gave Stephanie a sympathetic smile as she closed the front door.

Stephanie walked home, feeling worse than ever. She hung up her jacket on the hook by the front door and carried her backpack into the living room. Michelle skipped down the stairs.

"Hey, Stephanie, it's about time you got home," Michelle said. She waved a piece of paper in Stephanie's face. "Nathaniel called you again!"

Stephanie's heart skipped a beat. "Are you kidding?" she asked.

"Nope! You just missed him," Michelle replied. "He said he was going home, but that he was working tomorrow and you should call him then at the store."

"Really?" Stephanie beamed at Michelle. "He called me . . . twice! This is too good to believe!" she exclaimed. "I have to tell Darcy!" She reached for the phone and dialed Darcy's number.

"Stephanie! Guess what?" Darcy asked as soon as she answered the phone. "I won my tennis match today!"

"That's great," Stephanie told her.

"Yeah, I'm really happy!" Darcy paused. "But you know what else this means, don't you?"

"No, what?" Stephanie asked.

"My big loss, my big win—another one of Esther's predictions came true," Darcy said.

Stephanie groaned. "I'm beginning to wonder if she *can* predict the future after all."

She quickly told Darcy about Nathaniel's second phone call.

"This is wild!" Darcy exclaimed. "I mean, if Esther's predictions all come true, and you don't think she's a phony anymore, then Allie is right."

Stephanie took a deep breath. "Let's wait

and see what happens when I call Nathaniel tomorrow."

"I have a better idea," Darcy said. "Forget calling him back. I think you should go back to Beats and see him in person."

Stephanie thought for a moment. "That's a great idea, Darcy! Then I'll know for sure if Nathaniel is the one. And if Esther is one great fortune-teller or one great big fake!"

CHAPTER
11

◆ ◢ ◣ ◆

Stephanie was surprised to see Allie waiting by the pay phone the next morning at school. She crossed her fingers. *I hope my letter convinced Allie to forgive me.*

"Hey, Al," Stephanie called. "What's up?"

Allie glanced up from the book she was reading and smiled. "Hi, Stephanie," she said.

"You're speaking to me!" Stephanie cried in relief. "Listen, Allie," she began, "I am so incredibly sorry about the article. I never, ever meant to embarrass you. I can't believe I did that to my very best friend. It will never happen again, I promise!"

"I know that now," Allie told her.

"Great! Because I know it was a dumb thing to do," Stephanie went on. "I should have realized that everyone would know Ellie Tyler was Allie Taylor."

"That was pretty dumb," Allie agreed, smiling.

"I know, I know," Stephanie told her. "I'm so sorry! I'm just happy you're talking to me again. I thought we were finished being friends."

"Oh, I could never stay mad at you very long," Allie admitted. "You'll always be my best friend."

"And you'll always be mine," Stephanie told her. She paused. "And I have a confession to make. I'm starting to believe in Esther myself."

Allie's eyes widened. "You are?" she asked.

Stephanie nodded. "Maybe I should have waited before writing the article. I should have gotten my facts straight."

Allie grinned. "Now you're talking like a good friend—and a good journalist!"

The bell rang for class, and Allie put her arm around Stephanie's shoulders. "There's Darcy," she said, pointing down the hall. "Let's go tell her that we're friends again."

"And let's ask her if she'll come to the mall tonight with me and you," Stephanie said. "Because I need both my best friends around when I go to see Nathaniel!"

At dinner that night, Stephanie gobbled up her pasta. She glanced anxiously at Jesse. He had promised to drive her to the mall before leaving for his book discussion group that night.

Stephanie still hadn't gone over the ending of *The Tale of the Willow Tree* with him. But there would be time to explain the story in the car.

Stephanie checked the clock on the kitchen wall. It was six-thirty, and Darcy and Allie were meeting her at the mall at seven. She wished her family would hurry up and finish eating.

"So, Jesse," Danny said in between bites of linguini, "I hear your book group is discussing *The Tale of the Willow Tree* tonight."

"Mmmmphh," Jesse mumbled through a mouthful of pasta.

"That was such a great book," Joey said. He buttered a piece of Italian bread and took a bite.

"I cried my eyes out," Becky said. She paused to help Nicky wrap his linguini around his fork. "It was a real tearjerker."

"Remember when the little boy ran to the grandfather? Didn't you love that part?" Joey asked.

"Totally. What did you think, Jesse?" Danny asked.

All eyes turned to Jesse.

"Me? Oh, yeah, I thought it was real sad," Jesse said. "I never read such a sad thing before. I cried like a baby."

Everyone at the table was silent.

"You were sad, Jesse?" Becky asked.

Jesse twisted the last bit of pasta around his fork. "Completely," he replied. Then he noticed Becky staring strangely at him. Stephanie shot him a nervous look.

"What?" he asked. "Why are you looking at me that way?"

"Jesse, that part wasn't sad . . . it was happy!" Becky told him. "The boy realized his true love for his grandfather—it was beautiful! What did you find sad about that?"

Jesse quickly shoved the forkful of pasta into his mouth. "Mmmph . . . tears of happiness," Jesse mumbled. He pointed to his mouth and pretended he couldn't talk because it was full of food. He glanced at Stephanie.

"Oh, hey, Dad . . . that reminds me," Stephanie said, changing the subject. "I have a book report due in a few weeks on *The Catcher in the Rye*. Wasn't that your favorite book in school? Could you help me with my report?"

Danny put down his fork. "I'd love to, Steph! That was such a great book!"

Joey nodded. "The best! I read it at least ten times in high school and college."

Jesse swallowed his food and winked at Stephanie. "Thanks," he whispered. "Uh, we have to go," he told the others. He jumped up from the table and grabbed his car keys off the key rack. "I promised Stephanie I'd give her a ride to the mall."

Stephanie stood to follow him.

"Now, Stephanie," Danny said, "I don't want you home late. This is a school night, remember."

"I know, Dad," Stephanie said. "But Allie's mom is going to drive us home really early . . . I promise!"

Danny smiled. "Okay, as long as you don't make going out on a school night a regular thing."

Stephanie kissed him on the forehead. "I

won't," she said. She raced upstairs to her room to change. She tried on outfit after outfit. She finally settled on a short-sleeved black turtleneck and her denim miniskirt. She pulled on boots and black tights, then braided her hair in one long braid over her shoulder.

This outfit makes me look pretty cool, she thought. *Nathaniel will think I look like a girl who knows her alternative rock groups!*

Michelle came into the bedroom. She looked at the clothes strewn all over Stephanie's bed. "What are you all dressed up for?" Michelle asked. "Where are you going?"

"To meet someone," Stephanie said. She smoothed her bangs to the side and studied the effect in the mirror. She brushed her bangs to the other side.

"Someone special?" Michelle asked.

Stephanie glanced at her sister. "Michelle, this may be the most special person in my life!" Stephanie fluffed her bangs straight with her hand. She grabbed her backpack and flew down the back stairs.

Loud voices were arguing in the kitchen. Stephanie burst into the room. D.J.'s study group had arrived. They were all seated around the kitchen table, talking at once. Jake was there, too. When he saw Stephanie, he waved.

"Hey, Stephanie!" he called above the noise. "How are you doing?"

"Great," Stephanie said. She hurried to the fridge and poured herself a glass of juice. Thinking about seeing Nathaniel made her mouth feel dry.

Stephanie gulped down her juice and poured herself more. Out of the corner of her eye, she noticed Jake watching her. Jake *was* kind of cute. Not as cute as Nathaniel, but still cute. Of course, his name didn't begin with an *N*. She wasn't fated to be with a Jake.

"You guys don't have your facts straight!" D.J. nearly shouted at her friends. "Didn't you read the articles we were assigned?"

"We read them; we just don't agree on what they mean," one of the boys argued.

"You're both wrong," a dark-haired girl put in. "Those articles don't take sides. They're just important for the facts they contain."

Stephanie tuned the argument out. A tap on her shoulder startled her. It was Jake!

"Stephanie," Jake said loudly. "Can I ask you to read these articles?" he asked. "I think we need an outsider's opinion. These guys think they know everything."

"Hey, that's a good idea," D.J. put in. "Stephanie has some interesting ideas—sometimes." She raised her eyebrows at Stephanie.

Stephanie felt her face turn red. *I can't believe this*, she thought. *D.J. is trying to set me up with Jake!*

"So how about it, Stephanie?" Jake said. "But let's talk in the living room," he suggested. "I can't hear myself think in here."

Stephanie glanced at her watch. "Well, I have to leave soon. I'm waiting for my uncle Jesse. He's giving me a ride to the mall," she explained.

"You can talk until he's ready, can't you?" D.J. put in.

Stephanie cleared her throat and glared at D.J. She wasn't interested in Jake, but she didn't want to embarrass him in front of his friends. "Um, sure, I guess," she answered. Jake beamed at her.

Stephanie pushed through the swinging kitchen door. Jake followed her into the living room, and they both sat on the sofa. Stephanie glanced at her watch again.

Hurry, Uncle Jesse, she thought. *I don't want to miss Nathaniel!*

"So, where are these articles?" Stephanie asked. "You know, I hate to brag, but I write articles myself. For my school newspaper. The *Scribe*. I mean, it's not as good as your college paper, but I—"

"Stephanie, forget the articles," Jake told her. "That's not really why I asked you in here."

"Really?" Stephanie said.

Here it comes, she thought. *He's going to ask me out, like D.J. said!*

Jake glanced toward the kitchen door. "Well, it's about The Toners concert," he said.

"Right, The Toners," Stephanie said. "You know, Jake, The Toners are really pretty far out. And you know, well, most people really don't *like* alternative rock."

Jake smiled at her. "I know that. That's why it's so great that I met you. So, anyway, the concert is this weekend," he went on.

Stephanie glanced at her watch. Where was Uncle Jesse? They had to get to the mall before Nathaniel finished work for the night!

"The weekend?" Stephanie muttered. "That's still a pretty long time away," she added. "I mean, you have lots of time to make plans for the weekend."

"Not really," Jake said. "Though I'm pretty sure I can get tickets. But I just wanted to make sure of something before I made all the arrangements and everything," he added.

"You are so right!" Stephanie said. "I mean, what's the point of planning ahead if you aren't sure that the person you're thinking of asking actually wants to go someplace with you?" She gave Jake a bright smile.

"What?" Jake stared at her.

"Well, I mean, you should always leave time to ask *another* person—in case that person can't go for some reason," Stephanie finished.

"Right," Jake said. He gave her a puzzled look. "Uh, Stephanie—"

"I'm glad you mentioned The Toners," Stephanie interrupted. "Because, well, I don't like them anymore."

"You don't?" Jake frowned. "But you just told me you did. And you bought their new CD."

"Oh, that." Stephanie gave an airy wave of her hand. "I was wrong," she said. "You know how it is—you hear one song from a CD and *think* you like it. But then you listen again and it just doesn't cut it. Right?''

"Then I guess you're not interested in hearing them in concert," Jake said.

"Me? No way," Stephanie told him.

Jake looked really confused now. "I don't get it," he said. "D.J. told me to ask you out and—"

"Oh, did she? That D.J.!" Stephanie forced a chuckle. "What a sense of humor! After all, you're a college boy. Why would you want to go out with a girl who's only in middle school?"

"Well, because I—" Jake began to answer.

Stephanie heard footsteps coming down the stairs. A moment later, Uncle Jesse appeared, heading for the front door. "Ready, Steph?" he called. "Let's hit the mall. Don't forget, we have lots to talk about on the way!"

"Right!" Stephanie leaped off the couch. "Sorry, Jake!" she called over her shoulder. "I've got to run!"

Stephanie rushed through the front door and closed it behind her.

Whew! That was a close one, she thought. Now it was time to meet the boy who was right for her.

Nathaniel, Stephanie thought, *prepare to meet your fate—me, Stephanie!*

CHAPTER
12

◆ ◀ ◾ ◆

Jesse had already started the engine of the car. Stephanie climbed in and fastened her seat belt.

"All right!" Jesse exclaimed. "Now you've got to tell me what happens at the end of *The Tale of the Willow Tree!*"

"Okay! Okay!" Stephanie said. She took a deep breath. "Now, let me try and remember. . . ."

"You don't remember the story?" Jesse asked in alarm.

"Of course I do!" Stephanie said. "I don't remember where we left off."

"Right. Sorry," Jesse said. "We left off at the

part where the little boy tells the willow tree how much he loves it and the grandfather hears, then the little boy falls asleep under the tree."

Stephanie nodded. "Okay. Well, the little boy falls asleep under the tree. Then the story jumps ahead to when he's much older. His grandfather tells him how much he loves him. But the boy is playing with his friends, and he's embarrassed. He runs away from his grandfather. Then the boy realizes his grandfather's love is nothing to be ashamed about, and it's all because of the happy times they shared under the willow tree."

Jesse scrunched up his nose. "That's pretty dumb," he said.

"No, it isn't. It's beautiful," Stephanie told him.

Jesse made a face. "I'm just glad I didn't have to read it all myself!" Jesse glanced at his watch. "Hey, we'd better hurry. I've got to drop you off and get back to pick up Becky."

Stephanie shrugged. She didn't feel like talking anymore, anyway. All she really wanted to think about was Nathaniel. In just a few minutes, she would see her dream guy again! She felt almost dizzy with excitement.

Jesse pulled into the mall parking lot. "Hop out, Steph. I'm late!"

Stephanie jumped out and closed the car door. Jesse waved good-bye and pulled away. Stephanie hurried inside the mall. Darcy and Allie were already waiting at the Food Court. Stephanie rushed up to them. She was so nervous, her palms were all sweaty.

"Are you ready?" Darcy asked.

"I think so," Stephanie replied. "But what should I say? Or should I wait for him to say something first? Or should I make the first move?"

"Just play it cool," Darcy instructed. "Remember, he's called you twice already. That means he likes you!"

"And Esther predicted it," Allie added.

Stephanie nodded. "You're right. I have nothing to worry about." She smiled.

They hurried together through the mall to Beats. With each step, Stephanie's heart beat faster and faster. They reached the store, and Stephanie peered through the big glass window.

"That's him!" Stephanie exclaimed. She pointed toward Nathaniel. "There—he's helping a customer in the classical music section."

Stephanie could see Nathaniel sharing a laugh with the customer. Even from outside, his dimples showed when he smiled. And his eyes were so bright, they twinkled.

"Stephanie!" Darcy gaped. "He's gorgeous!"

"I told you," Stephanie replied.

"Wow, Steph!" Allie added. "He's about the cutest guy I've ever seen!"

Stephanie suddenly felt as if a ten-pound weight had landed on her chest. "I think I'm losing my nerve," she managed to say. "Maybe we should leave. . . ."

Nathaniel glanced up and spotted her through the window. He shot her a quick smile, then turned back to his customer.

"He saw you!" Darcy said. "You can't leave now. Just walk up to him and wait for him to finish with his customer. And remember . . . play it cool!"

Stephanie gulped. "Easy for you to say," she muttered. "Come inside with me, you guys," she said.

"Okay. And don't worry," Allie told her. "This is in the stars."

Darcy and Allie followed Stephanie into the

store. Stephanie headed toward Nathaniel, trying to keep a calm smile on her face.

Stay cool, she reminded herself. *This is it . . . Esther said it would happen, and it's happening! I'm about to talk to the guy of my dreams. My destiny!*

She cleared her throat. "Uh, Nathaniel! Hi!" she managed to say.

Nathaniel turned and gazed at her. He seemed confused for a minute, then he broke into a smile. "Hey! What's up?" he said.

"Great. How are you?" Stephanie asked.

"Great." Nathaniel smiled at Stephanie, then at Darcy and Allie. "I'll be right with you," he told them. He turned back to the man he was helping.

Stephanie shot a giddy look at her friends as they waited for Nathaniel. Finally he finished with his customer and turned to face them again.

"I'm glad you came back," Nathaniel told Stephanie. "There's something I wanted to tell you."

Stephanie felt lightheaded. "Nathaniel!" she blurted. "I . . . I feel the same way about you!"

Nathaniel stared at her as if she were from Mars. "Huh?" he asked. "Feel the same way about what?"

Stephanie blinked. "Well, about that I should have explained why I couldn't come back to the store that evening," she said. "I hope you didn't think I didn't want to. It's just that my uncle was waiting, and I couldn't stay. But then when you called me . . . twice! . . . I knew I had to come talk to you in person so you wouldn't think—"

Nathaniel held up a hand. "Whoa! Hang on a second," he said. "I mean, you look very familiar, but I'm a little confused."

A sick feeling began to build in Stephanie's stomach. *I look familiar?* she wondered. *Doesn't he recognize me?*

"You . . . you don't know who I am?" she asked.

Nathaniel frowned. "Well, I know we've met, but I'm not sure why you're here."

Stephanie felt her face turn red-hot. "You . . . you called me," she said. "Last night and the night before. I was in here on Sunday—you sold me The Toners' new CD. . . ."

Nathaniel broke into a smile again. "Oh, right!" he said. "You forgot to fill out the back of the form."

"Form?" Stephanie repeated.

"Sure—for our mailing list," Nathaniel told

her. "My manager asked me to call you and get the rest of your address."

"That's why you called?" Stephanie asked.

Nathaniel nodded. "Yeah, I realized it right after you left. But you did write your phone number, so I called you. Hey, you didn't have to come all the way down here, you know. I just wanted you to call."

"Oh, I, uh, believe in filling out forms in person," Stephanie said.

Nathaniel hurried over to the cash register. He found the form in a drawer and brought it back to Stephanie. She filled in her address and zip code and handed it back to Nathaniel.

"Thanks," he said. "Now I can notify you of our next big sale!"

"Great," Stephanie said. She backed away from Nathaniel and turned to Darcy and Allie. "Let's get out of here," she whispered. "I've never been so embarrassed in my whole life!"

Stephanie walked out of the store as calmly as she could. Allie and Darcy followed her back to the Food Court. Stephanie collapsed onto an empty chair. "Tell me that just didn't happen!" she exclaimed.

"I'm afraid it did," Darcy said.

"I can't believe what a jerk I was," Stephanie went on. "Thinking he called because he liked me! He didn't even *recognize* me!"

Stephanie dropped her face into her hands. "I'm so embarrassed! I can never shop in that store again!"

"I'm really sorry, Steph," Allie said.

Stephanie groaned. "And the worst part is, that guy Jake *did* like me! He even asked me to a concert this weekend."

"Well, that's great," Darcy told her. "Then you have something to be happy about. I mean, who needs Nathaniel when you have Jake?"

"But I don't have Jake!" Stephanie exclaimed. "I turned him down. I thought I'd be going out with Nathaniel!"

"Wow. And now you don't have anybody. What a mess," Darcy said.

"Don't worry, Steph," Allie told her. "Esther is never wrong. She probably meant for you to meet some *other* N guy!"

"Esther was *too* wrong!" Stephanie exclaimed. "I never should have listened to her dumb prediction! This is the worst night of my life, and it's all Esther's fault!"

"It is not," Allie insisted.

Stephanie glanced at Darcy, then back at Allie. "Allie, you're my friend," Stephanie began. "And I don't want to fight with you again. But do me one favor—" Stephanie paused and took a deep breath. "Don't ever mention Esther's name again!"

CHAPTER
13

♦ ◂ ◢ ♦

Mrs. Taylor dropped Stephanie in front of her house. Stephanie let herself in and plodded up the stairs to her room. She flung open the door and threw herself onto her bed.

"What a terrible night!" Stephanie groaned.

Michelle sat up in her bed and stared. "What happened?" she asked.

"You wouldn't understand," Stephanie told her. "This night is a total bust. I'm going to go right to sleep."

Stephanie changed into pajamas and hurried down the hall to wash up and brush her teeth.

When she got back to her bedroom, D.J. was sitting on her bed, waiting for her.

"What's up, Deej?" Stephanie asked. She plopped down on the bed next to D.J.

"That's what I'd like to know," D.J. said. "What did you do to Jake, anyway?"

Stephanie gulped. "I didn't do anything."

"But I told him to ask you out," D.J. said. "And then you turned him down! He was so embarrassed, and I felt like an idiot!"

"Sorry, Deej," Stephanie muttered.

Michelle piped up. "A college boy wanted to go out with Stephanie?" she asked in disbelief.

"Be quiet, Michelle!" Stephanie turned to D.J. "It wasn't my fault," she said. "It's just that Jake's name doesn't begin with an *N*."

"What are you talking about?" D.J. stared at her.

"Esther! It's all *her* fault!" Stephanie punched her pillow. "She made me do it! I made a huge mistake, and now I feel so dumb! Stupid, stupid, stupid!"

"Who is Esther?" D.J. asked.

"And why are you punching your pillow?" Michelle added.

"Because I should have my head examined!" Stephanie said.

"Steph, slow down," D.J. told her. "I can't follow you."

Stephanie swallowed. "Esther is a fortune-teller. She said I was going to meet the guy of my dreams," she explained. "She said he'd have the initial N. So I met this guy named Nathaniel. And he really seemed to like me."

"What's that got to do with Jake?" D.J. asked.

"That's why I wouldn't go out with Jake," Stephanie replied. "I thought I'd have a date with Nathaniel this weekend. Because he has an N name."

D.J. shook her head. "No offense, Steph," she said. "But that was really dumb of you."

"I know that now." Stephanie flopped onto her back and stared up at the ceiling. "I will never listen to a fortune-teller again," she said. "I'm back to being a complete nonbeliever—believe it!"

There was a knock on the bedroom door. Uncle Jesse barged into the room. His face was flushed red with anger.

"Thanks a lot, Stephanie!" he told her.

Stephanie sat up and stared at him in confusion. "Why do you look so mad?" she asked.

Jesse put his hands on his hips. "Thanks to you, Becky isn't speaking to me! And I was totally humiliated in front of our whole discussion group!"

"But what did I do?" Stephanie asked.

"It's what you *didn't* do!" Jesse told her. "You never told me the very end of *The Tale of the Willow Tree!*"

"I did!" Stephanie insisted. "I told you everything that happened to the boy and his grandpa."

"But you left out the most important part," Jesse said. "The part where the old willow tree has to be chopped down because it has a disease."

Stephanie gasped. "You're right! Oh, Uncle Jesse, I meant to tell you the ending. But you started saying how dumb the story was and then—well, I guess I forgot that part."

Jesse threw up his hands. "Is that all you can say? You forgot?"

"I . . . I guess so. I had a lot on my mind," Stephanie added. "I was thinking about what this fortune-teller said and stuff."

"Well, I told everyone in the group that I loved the book's happy ending, and they laughed in my face," Jesse said. "Now Becky's so embarrassed that she won't speak to me."

"Sorry, Uncle Jesse," Stephanie murmured.

"Next time I think about making a deal with you, remind me *not* to!" Jesse said. He spun around and marched out of the room.

Stephanie flopped back onto her bed.

D.J. and Michelle stared at her. "Sounds like you messed up twice tonight," Michelle said.

"Wow, Steph, you'd better get this whole fortune-teller thing straightened out in your mind," D.J. said. "Or you might get in even bigger trouble."

"You're right," Stephanie replied. "And I know just the place to start!

Stephanie ran down the hall after Jesse.

"Uncle Jesse, wait!" she called. Jesse stopped in his tracks. "I really *am* sorry about the book," Stephanie told him. "I should have paid more attention to you and not been thinking about dumb fortunes."

Jesse frowned. "Hold on, Steph," he said. "Maybe it's not your fault. I'm sorry, too."

"You are?" Stephanie asked in surprise.

"Yeah. I did cut you off. I guess it was all a misunderstanding. And I shouldn't have cheated in the first place," he said. "I know you were really trying to help."

"Then you're not mad at me anymore?" Stephanie asked.

"Nope." Jesse gave Stephanie a hug. "Are you mad at me?"

"Nope." Stephanie grinned.

"Great. Now all I have to do is find Becky and apologize like crazy." Jesse crossed his fingers. "Wish me luck!" He hurried up the stairs to the attic.

Allie and Darcy were already waiting by the pay phone the next morning as Stephanie ran up.

"Hi, guys!" Stephanie greeted them. "Sorry I'm late!"

"That's okay," Darcy told her. "But we're dying to find out how you are after everything that happened with Jake and Nathaniel yesterday."

"Don't ask!" Stephanie said. "But you know, I'm kind of glad it happened."

Allie and Darcy exchanged confused looks. "Why are you glad?" Darcy asked.

"Because it opened my eyes," Stephanie answered. "It made me see that it was my fault. It was dumb of me to put so much faith in Esther's prediction."

"Well, it's all pretty confusing. Esther *was* right about a lot of things," Darcy said.

"But was she?" Stephanie asked. "Think about it. The thing about me having the key to the van and Darcy losing her earring could have been coincidence."

"What about your winning that money with clown number four?" Allie asked.

"That could have been another coincidence," Stephanie said. "I *am* good at that game."

"That's true," Darcy said.

"And you're a great tennis player," Stephanie pointed out. "You might have won no matter what Esther said."

"I guess that's true, too," Darcy admitted.

"Anyway, no one can prove it one way or the other," Stephanie said. "That's why you guys have to come with me tonight."

"Come where with you?" Allie asked.

"To see Esther," Stephanie answered. "And this time, we're not asking for predictions— we're asking for the truth."

CHAPTER
14

◆ ◀ ◗ ◆

"Esther, we need to talk!" Stephanie announced as she pushed through the flaps of Esther's Tent of Wonder.

Esther glanced up from her fortune-telling cards and smiled. "Stephanie!" she said. "I had a feeling you'd be back again." Her smile faded as she glanced at Stephanie's serious expression. "Is there something wrong?" she asked.

"Yes, there's something wrong," Stephanie said. "I don't think it's right for you to pretend to know things if you don't really know them."

Esther stacked her cards into a neat pile, then

motioned for Stephanie, Darcy, and Allie to sit down.

"I never pretend I know everything," Esther said. "I just try to understand what cards or horoscopes *might* mean. I think of myself as giving advice—not the absolute truth."

"But that's the problem," Stephanie told her. "I mean, you can't really prove if what you say is true or not. And that's dangerous."

"Oh, I never tell anyone to do something that might be dangerous," Esther said.

"But you did," Stephanie replied. "I mean, Allie believed your predictions completely. She practically wouldn't leave the house without reading her horoscope or calling The Psychic Hot Line to make sure it was safe!"

"And she spent all her allowance on fortune-telling stuff," Darcy added.

"And she wouldn't talk to us for one whole day because she thought we had bad vibes," Stephanie said.

Allie flushed. "I guess I did go a little overboard," she said.

"And don't forget how you almost cut school to avoid bad karma," Darcy reminded her.

"Stop!" Esther said. She looked straight at Allie. "Did you really do all those things?"

"Well, yeah," Allie admitted. "At first so many of your predictions came true."

"Don't get me wrong, Allie," Esther said. "I believe in the science of astrology. And I love reading cards and palms. But fortune-telling isn't my whole life. Actually, I work at a bank during the day."

"You do?" Allie stared at Esther in shock. "I don't get it," she said. "I thought you really had some kind of special powers."

"I can't prove if I do or I don't," Esther told her. "It's up to you to decide that."

"But how did you know so much about us?" Darcy asked.

Esther smiled. "Don't tell anyone else, but some of what I say comes from watching people."

Esther gestured at Darcy. "For instance, your varsity jacket. It says John Muir Middle School Tennis Club. You also have a tennis racket charm and a hockey stick charm on your bracelet," Esther explained.

Darcy touched her charm bracelet. "That's right!" she said. "I always wear these."

"So it wasn't hard to figure out that you're an athlete," Esther told her.

"That sounds like a trick!" Allie exclaimed.

"Well, it is, sort of, I guess," Esther replied.

"How did you know I was an animal lover?" Allie asked.

"Your jacket was covered with animal hairs," Esther told her. "From holding your pet dog or cat, I guessed. Was I right?"

Allie's face reddened. "My two cats," she said. "I always forget to clean my jacket before I go out!"

Esther winked. "Sometimes I just guess, too," she said.

Stephanie frowned. "Why did you tell me that stuff about a boy with the initial *N*? That he'd declare his love for me? I mean, it wasn't true—and I really embarrassed myself because I believed you."

Esther shrugged. "But, Stephanie, I predicted it might happen in your *future*. You have many, many years of future ahead of you. It could *still* happen!"

Esther dug into her pocket. She handed Darcy, Allie, and Stephanie their money back. "Here— no hard feelings," she told them.

"No hard feelings," Stephanie told her.

She, Darcy, and Allie left the tent. Darcy paused outside the doorway, gazing at the long line of people waiting to go in. "I wonder if all those people will believe Esther's predictions," she said.

"Who knows?" Stephanie answered. "I'm just glad I don't have to live my life according to what someone else tells me to do."

"Me too," Allie said.

Stephanie and Darcy looked at Allie in surprise. "Do you mean that?" Stephanie asked.

Allie gave a sheepish grin. "Yeah. I was about to give up on the whole fortune-telling thing myself."

"You were?" Stephanie asked. "Why?"

Allie flushed in embarrassment. "My mom got the telephone bill yesterday, and she threw a major fit. Did you know that every call to The Psychic Hot Line costs twelve dollars?"

Darcy's eyes widened in shock. "Wow! That's a fortune!" she said.

"How many calls did you make?" Stephanie asked.

Allie gulped. "About twenty," she mumbled.

"Twenty?" Stephanie screeched. She added

quickly in her head. "That's almost two hundred and fifty dollars!"

"I know," Allie replied. "My parents are furious. I'm not getting my allowance for two months—I have to help pay for the calls."

"Ouch. That hurts," Stephanie said.

"You're telling me," Allie replied. "And I'm also grounded for two whole weekends. For pretending to be sick on Monday," she added.

"They found out about that, huh?" Stephanie asked.

"Yeah," Allie said. "My mom asked me about the closet shelf that we left on the floor, and I confessed."

Stephanie shook her head again. "I'll bet *that* wasn't in your horoscope."

"Nope," Allie admitted. "And there's something else I didn't tell you." She flushed. "Wait until you see this," she said.

Allie reached into her backpack and pulled out a sheet of paper. "Check this out. I got an A on my big history test. The one Esther said would be bad luck."

"An A! Allie, that's great!" Stephanie exclaimed. "Why didn't you tell us before?"

"I was too embarrassed," Allie admitted. "I studied extra hard for this test and did great. That proves it had nothing to do with luck, good or bad.

"I'm just glad that you worried for nothing," Stephanie said.

"Thanks. I'm sorry, you guys," Allie said. "I don't know why I got so carried away."

"It could happen to anyone," Stephanie told her. "Look how I believed Esther about the *N* guy! But at least we all learned our lesson. No fortune-teller can tell you how to live your life."

Stephanie glanced at her watch. It was almost time to meet Jesse for their ride home. "We'd better head over to the bottle toss game to meet Uncle Jesse," Stephanie said. They began walking past the game booths.

"Is Jesse still mad at you about the book?" Darcy asked.

Stephanie shook her head. "No, we made up. He said it was really his fault for cheating in the first place," she said. "And he knew I really was trying to help."

"Is Becky still mad at him?" Allie asked.

"No, I think they made up, too," Stephanie said. "Hey! There they are!" She pointed ahead. Aunt Becky and Uncle Jesse were already at the game booth with the twins.

As Stephanie hurried up to them Jesse helped Alex toss some colored hoops at a stack of bottles. The hoops all missed. Stephanie lifted Nicky to play the game.

"Your turn, Nicky!" Stephanie said. "I'll help you win one for the family. You can do it, I know you can!"

Nicky aimed, then tossed a red hoop. Stephanie held her breath as it sailed through the air.

Clank!

The hoop landed around the neck of a bottle! There was a moment of stunned silence.

"He did it!" Becky cried in disbelief.

"He did it!" Jesse repeated.

"I won! I won!" Nicky cried.

Stephanie, Darcy, and Allie cheered. Jesse lifted Alex up to Nicky, and the twins slapped their hands together in a high five. The woman working the booth handed Nicky a small stuffed monkey. Nicky's face lit up.

"I won a monkey! Thanks, Cousin Stephanie," he said. "You helped me win. I love you!" Nicky leaned over to wrap his arm around Stephanie's neck. He hugged her tight.

Stephanie squeezed him back. "I love you, too, Nicky," she said.

Stephanie glanced over at Allie and Darcy. They gaped back at her in amazement.

"What, you guys? What's wrong?" Stephanie asked.

"He . . . you . . . it's . . ." Allie stuttered.

"You don't get it, do you?" Darcy cried in delight.

"Get what?" Stephanie frowned in confusion.

"It's Nicky! Your *N* guy!" Darcy cried. "He just vowed his love for you!"

"And you said that you love him back," Allie said.

Stephanie's mouth dropped open. "I don't believe it," she said. "Esther was right!"

"I don't know what you guys are talking about," Jesse told them. "But since you helped Nicky win the game, I'm going to treat you all to one last carnival ride."

"All right!" Stephanie cheered. She handed Nicky to Jesse and took off running.

Darcy and Allie chased after her. "Steph, wait!" Darcy called.

"I can't wait—my prediction won't come true," Stephanie called back.

"What prediction?" Allie asked.

Stephanie laughed. "I predict that I'm going to beat both of you guys to the Ferris wheel!"

FULL HOUSE™
Stephanie

PHONE CALL FROM A FLAMINGO	88004-7/$3.99
THE BOY-OH-BOY NEXT DOOR	88121-3/$3.99
TWIN TROUBLES	88290-2/$3.99
HIP HOP TILL YOU DROP	88291-0/$3.99
HERE COMES THE BRAND NEW ME	89858-2/$3.99
THE SECRET'S OUT	89859-0/$3.99
DADDY'S NOT-SO-LITTLE GIRL	89860-4/$3.99
P.S. FRIENDS FOREVER	89861-2/$3.99
GETTING EVEN WITH THE FLAMINGOES	52273-6/$3.99
THE DUDE OF MY DREAMS	52274-4/$3.99
BACK-TO-SCHOOL COOL	52275-2/$3.99
PICTURE ME FAMOUS	52276-0/$3.99
TWO-FOR-ONE CHRISTMAS FUN	53546-3/$3.99
THE BIG FIX-UP MIX-UP	53547-1/$3.99
TEN WAYS TO WRECK A DATE	53548-X/$3.99
WISH UPON A VCR	53549-8/$3.99
DOUBLES OR NOTHING	56841-8/$3.99
SUGAR AND SPICE ADVICE	56842-6/$3.99
NEVER TRUST A FLAMINGO	56843-4/$3.99
THE TRUTH ABOUT BOYS	00361-5/$3.99
CRAZY ABOUT THE FUTURE	00362-3/$3.99

Available from Minstrel® Books Published by Pocket Books

Simon & Schuster Mail Order Dept. BWB
200 Old Tappan Rd., Old Tappan, N.J. 07675

Please send me the books I have checked above. I am enclosing $_____(please add $0.75 to cover the postage and handling for each order. Please add appropriate sales tax). Send check or money order--no cash or C.O.D.'s please. Allow up to six weeks for delivery. For purchase over $10.00 you may use VISA: card number, expiration date and customer signature must be included.

Name _____

Address _____

City _____ State/Zip _____

VISA Card # _____ Exp.Date _____

Signature _____

929-19